PICKING AT THE KNOT

Sarah Hampton

2QT Limited (Publishing)

First Edition published 2016 by

2QT Limited (Publishing)
Settle
North Yorkshire
BD24 9RH
United Kingdom

Picking at the Knot is a work of fiction and any resemblance
to any person living or dead is purely coincidental

Cover Design: Hilary Pitt
Cover images: shutterstock.com

Printed in Great Britain by Lightning Source UK

A CIP catalogue record for this book is available
from the British Library

ISBN 978-1-910077-99-3

For my beloved Great Grandson, whose birthday I have trouble remembering, with the hope that he will, in his own time, question the status quo.

ACKNOWLEDGEMENTS

My thanks to Catherine Cousins at 2QT for her faith and help in publishing my second novel. To Karen Holmes, my dear friend, mentor and editor, who has encouraged me throughout and kept me on the straight and narrow. Special thanks to my neighbours and friends, whose kindness and support enable me to remain living in the place I love.

I have longed to move away
From the hissing of the spent lie
And the old terrors' continual cry
Growing more terrible as the day
Goes over the hill into the deep sea;
I have longed to move away
From the repetition of salutes,
For there are ghosts in the air
And ghostly echoes on paper,
And the thunder of calls and notes.

I have longed to move away but am afraid
Some life, yet unspent, might explode
Out of the old lie burning on the ground,
And, crackling into the night air, leave me half-blind.
Neither by night's ancient fear,
The parting of hat from hair,
Pursed lips at the receiver,
Shall I fall to death's feather?
By these I would not wish to die,
Half convention and half lie.

Dylan Thomas – 1914–1953

CHAPTER 1

He lay spread-eagled. His left hand felt the unforgiving hardness of the concrete and he heard again his father's voice shout, 'You've been bloody useless from the day you were born.'

The pain had not been immediate. He lay on his back, the morning sky a wash of watery greys fusing into one another, threatening black to delicate silver, the morning pink of the sun already gone. Now its low yellow laser shaft was penetrating his eyes. He did not want to close them and curtain the beauty. He tried to move his head but it would not obey him.

An aircraft's white vapour trail dissected the sun's ray. He had never been in an aeroplane, never witnessed the other side. Never seen beyond the clouds, seen the beauty of nothingness, other than in his imagination.

He tried to move his right hand and felt the curled, frozen crispness of a leaf beneath it. He could see its beauty in his head, shell-shaped, silver cloaked in the night's late spring frost.

Stillness engulfed him. Far away he heard the persistent get-out-of-my-way, get-out-of-my-way wail of an ambulance. His body was lifted, a kindly word was spoken, the prick of a needle.

1

An authoritarian voice, not his dead father's: 'Middle-aged male, multiple fractures, suspected spinal damage. Fell through a barn roof, answers to Matt.' Then welcome oblivion, drifting back to a softer landing.

On his back in the newly cut hayfield, the breath knocked out of him, the familiar sweetness of the new-mown meadow hay in his nostrils. Beneath his small outstretched hand he felt a clover head which had escaped the cutter. Waiting for the bees to suck its nectar as he had been shown to do by his mother, recalling that minute sweetness between his lips.

On that day the sky was bright blue and cloudless, the sun blinding in its midday supremacy. He had been hanging on to the torn pocket of his father's coat, the only security on offer. On the other side of father's body, the warm pink hand of his three-year-old sister Carla, two years his junior, was being squeezed tightly. Father was looking down at her, smiling, chatting.

Something dislodged his grasp; he saw again his father's elbow move forward then change direction with certainty and speed.

He got to his feet, panting, and fell in behind, frightened to go too close. He thought of returning to the house to seek solace from his mother but indoors the farmhouse was cold and dark; outside the sun gave him a warmth and comfort and he wanted to see the new-born calf. That was the reason they were crossing the field where his favourite cow had given birth to a bull calf.

Had his birth given his father any pleasure? He wished he could remember the day he was born. Were toasts drunk to a first-born son? Was there pride in his father's eyes, someone to carry on the farm? But somehow it had gone wrong; he had become a disappointment but he didn't know why.

No one in the family had been ready for him. By the time he understood the sly whisperings, shotgun marriage, wrong side of the blanket, he had become the product of resentment. Not from his mother, who was even-handed when dealing with him and his sister, who put herself out to protect him and by that act incurred her husband's wrath.

'Turning him into a bloody namby-pamby.'

Time hushed the whisperings but the scar they left had deepened. He had tried to ignore the buried rejection but it rose to the surface from time to time and enveloped him.

At Christmas time, when other families were jolly and he still had hope on his side, his mother had asked, 'What would you like Santa Claus to bring you?'

'A little paint box and a brush.'

His father heard and shouted, 'Only pooftas want paint boxes.'

His sister's request for a Barbie doll with its sickly-pink lifestyle had been granted. He had not understood, for things not understood are more easily accepted.

As the years passed he watched his sister's contrived social climb. There she was, her picture in the paper: local woman gives her all for charity. That seeking after fame was encouraged by her being entered in a beauty competition at the local agricultural show by their father. At the age of six, Carla was Miss Dairy Queen, 1962.

Lying between the unfamiliar crispness of newly laundered white sheets, Matt wondered who had found him and reported the accident; he rarely had visitors and the postman infrequently left mail in the tin box at the bottom of the lane. Perhaps one of Matt's neighbours had a drone; he had heard about such things on TV.

He had lain in clean white sheets once before on his honeymoon in an unfamiliar hotel, because that was what was expected of him. But on the return to the farm, reality had taken control once more and his wife had left. He wondered: if she heard that there had been an accident, would she come? Once upon a time they had loved; people said he had driven her away. They had married too young but he hadn't felt that. He had been overwhelmed when that gentle soul said yes and then left within six months.

Had he been too rough with her, subjecting her innocence to farmhouse ways? But he remembered revering her butterfly-body, a wisp of soft deliciousness beneath his rough, gnarled hands grown large through necessity and evolution to become what was required of them. His physical longing and his strength were held back by respect for her.

When she left him, he should have left, gone to London, been a street artist. He had heard there was some guy called Banksy down there who painted on walls unseen in the night, slept rough, away from censure and ridicule, watching anonymously in the shadows as his work was acclaimed and gave pleasure to people. Matt would have enjoyed that and escaped the further ridicule of his father's remarks: 'Couldn't even hold onto a woman.'

Instead, to try and prove himself in some way, Matt had hastily remarried – and then he had left her.

He stayed on at the farm out of loyalty and duty to

support his mother and help his father, for he had been taught nothing else. His mother's death certificate said 'pulmonary embolism' but he knew she had died of a broken heart.

He lay between clean white sheets, smelling alien chemical smells in conflict with nature, manufactured to keep it at bay. His mother had loved the honest pungent smell of manure being spread on the crisp frozen earth, the muck spreader flinging its contents to replenish and enrich the soil. 'Nature's confetti,' she called it. Now there were complaints from second-home owners and holidaymakers who didn't like the smell.

Matt lay immobile, confused. A kind smiling face asked him how he was feeling then turned to a group of white-coated, eager young people with clipboards. They were being asked questions about him. He would have liked to join in, help them out, but that didn't seem to be part of what was expected of him so he lay there listening.

'X-rays reveal multiple old fractures behind the current ones, set by unqualified hands. The bones have strengthened themselves, readjusted without medical intervention to form strong misshapen joints.'

As the doctors and students left the ward, the bedside TVs were switched on again – patients trying to catch up with the real world which they had left outside. An obese middle-aged man in the bed opposite asked if anyone had seen last night's episode of *EastEnders*; he had missed it whilst he was having his stomach bypass operation. His TV flickered for a moment on the wrong channel; there was a glimpse of skeletal Somalian children, runny noses and eyes covered with flies, their ballooning bellies competing for attention. The man swore at the zapper, finally got back to Jeremy Kyle and settled down to watch something he understood.

In the bed to his right was a young man with an iPod in his ear, his open pyjama jacket exposing his beer belly. The pyjama bottoms were printed with transfers of naked girls, almost full size, looking up towards his crotch. In place of hair, his shaven head sported a confusion of tattoos; where eyebrows had once been there was a graded line of studs. His nose was heavily bandaged. He was reading a copy of *Nuts*. On his bedside locker there were other similar magazines, a can of lager and some crisps.

The pretty duty nurse remonstrated and received abuse: 'It's my rights,' the man said then told her to F off.

Matt drifted off to sleep again until he was woken by a crash. The tattooed patient was out of bed and was trying to swat a honeybee with the rolled-up copy of *Nuts*. The bee was buzzing frantically against the window, having inadvertently lost its way and flown into the warmth of the ward to escape the cold. It was heavily laden, its two yellow paniers of pollen making flight cumbersome, instinct telling it to escape and finish its task.

Matt shouted, 'Leave it alone!'

'Don't you bloody tell me what to do!'

Matt drained the water from his glass, pushed Tattoos onto his bed and captured the bee against the window with the tumbler, slipping the instruction card for the TV entertainment system between the rim of the glass and window pane. The bee buzzed angrily for a few seconds before Matt released it through the open window. He wished he could have gone with it.

Tomorrow, if the pain was not too bad, he would discharge himself as he had always done in the past. He would make a comfrey poultice to wrap around his shattered femur. The bone would eventually heal; it might be deformed but nature would deal with it.

Anyway, he had no choice. His livestock needed to be fed and there was no one else to call upon. The young school leavers came for a day's work experience, did nothing other than complain about getting their hands dirty, and he was getting married again on Tuesday.

Chapter 2

The young swallows were circling the kitchen, twittering excitedly, testing their wings, exploring to see what was inside the dark of the open door. They wheeled so fast that they were in and out before Julia was aware of them. They were learning to take their meals on the wing, sweeping low to catch the early morning midges, still under the reassuring tweet of their mother's call.

Usually she remembered to keep the back door closed when the swallows fledged; the youngsters, discovering flight and freedom from the cramped nest and squabbling siblings, often took wrong turns in the exuberance of youth,

Julia could hear Hugh's voice shouting, 'Why didn't you close the bloody door?' Despite his death, she was still within his orbit, her mind programmed to accept blame, daily making an effort not to do those things of which he would have disapproved.

She had lasted far longer as a widow than she had wished for or anticipated. She had become a statistic, processed by state, spouted about at budget time and wooed when her vote was needed. It was not a category she would have chosen. If she was still around in two years' time, and if the royal family hadn't abdicated, she might receive a congratulatory card from King Charles, or maybe King

William. The prospect did not thrill her.

Every morning she awoke worrying about the state of the world, parasitic thoughts feeding on her mind. In some ways she felt she had adapted rather well to a world so completely changed from the one she had been taught to trust and accept. She felt that she was a sapling still, swaying in a stiff breeze, trying to bend to the harsh winds of change to which her few remaining friends had succumbed; they had buried their minds in the sand, retreated back into the certainty of youth, unable to move forward.

Nine billion of us, so the media statistics informed her, a swarm of humans munching and fracking away at Earth, devouring the planet until only the skeletal remains would remain. Dear old David Attenborough had said as much way back in 2013: 'Curb the population or become extinct.' Few had listened and the age of profligacy dawned, when image was all and substance no longer mattered.

Julia heard again her mother's angry voice of chastisement as she, Julia, helped in the kitchen when she was eleven years old. She had drained the water from the boiled vegetables down the sink, thinking she was helping. Mother shouted that it should have gone into the stock pot, regurgitated to give future sustenance when wartime survival was all and people pulled together.

Julia knew she was drinking too much but felt it was in a good cause.

Now nothing was allowed its natural lifespan: scientists, medicine and do-gooders were determined to keep everything animate alive, whether the recipients of their interference and intervention wanted it or not. A sentimental public had even been conned into financing themed care homes to continue the suffering of sick animals.

The young no longer sought the wisdom of elder statesmen. The process had been reversed; the art of communication had been expunged, usurped, overgrown by the creeping bindweed of twittering digital observations. Elders imparting knowledge and guidance to the young were abhorred. Julia, born of an age which had made sure that children were seen and not heard, was experiencing the same dismissal in old age.

There had been a fleeting moment over a decade ago, when she was in her early eighties, when people had listened and been interested in what she could contribute. She had published a book and it had been shortlisted for a well-known literary award. After the congratulations, it disappeared quickly off the radar.

God, she thought, had made a bad choice: Homo sapiens were too clever by half and He probably knew it; mankind was bloody nasty. He had already given a warning of how it might turn out when He created that garden in Eden. And those Victorian hymn writers, so ridiculed and reviled by clever chat-show hosts who hoped for a quick laugh at the expense of someone else's beliefs, were spot on when they wrote 'Every Prospect pleases and only man is vile'. Perhaps John Lennon was the New Messiah and we had been too afraid to recognise him, too uncertain of ourselves to speak up.

Julia was unsure where these revelations were coming from. She noticed that her litre bottle of Famous Grouse had gone down alarmingly quickly over the past two days.

God should have chosen a different species to spread

the word of harmony and love: honey bees would have been good alternative – hardworking, community spirited, spreading happiness and dying when their job was done. Now God's options to correct His mistake were running out; all He had left to call upon to take man back to a new beginning were the four horsemen of the Apocalypse.

She closed the door to stop the swallows exploring further. Once, they had made it upstairs and, panicking, had messed in a bedroom. Today one was thrashing, its wings beating against the kitchen window, trapped, seeing its world and the sky through the prison of a glass pane in her kitchen.

Julia stretched out her hand and saw terror in its eyes but its flailing wings stilled under her restraining hold. No more struggling to escape, only the rapid pounding of a tiny heart in her hand, its thistledown weight belying its strength. It was a steely blue, chestnut and white dandelion head of feathers waiting to be released on the wind. She held her hands to the sky and neither felt nor saw the bird go. She wanted to say goodbye, wish it well on its journey to Africa. She hoped it would fly high and keep going, avoid the mist-netting and lime-sticking and tape, and not be lured down by a need for rest to become a delicacy on some Frenchman's plate.

Its fragility reminded her of Harry, her late-in-the-day last grandchild. How lucky she was to have him. What an unexpected bonus at the end of life; it was his mind that kept hers youthful.

As a fledgling, he had taken wrong turns. Feeling the heartbeat of the swallow she felt again the pulse in Harry's small hand, clasping hers as they went for walks. They had

11

gone to the lower slopes of Gowbarrow, the enchanted secret garden of her youth, the hillside carpeted in russet-coloured autumn bracken, narrow trods, cropped short by sheep's teeth and walkers' feet, dotted with sheep and rabbit droppings among the head-high bracken and glimpses of Ullswater below.

'Are we in the jungle, Granny?' Pulling her arm. 'Let's climb to the top of that mountain, Granny.'

Because he could not understand the restrictions of old age, he did not understand when she said no. He let go of her hand, raced ahead and disappeared down a dip in the land, coming again into her sight as he climbed further upwards where the bracken had become sparse. Out of hearing, his excited chatter changed into the distant muffled roar of Aira Force.

And Julia remembered her brothers stripped naked, jumping from the slender grey-slate bridge which spanned the torrent into the foaming peaty pool beneath, gasping at the coldness and the thrill of it in that enchanted time when, as children, they had believed that Ullswater belonged to them. A time when adventure was unfenced and unsignposted, and Nellie the cook made them egg sandwiches in case they got peckish and told them to drink the water upstream of any dead sheep they might find in the beck. Riding the eight miles on their bikes, Julia trying to keep up with her older brothers, leaving their bikes by the roadside and walking up the field till they came to their private magical world before the tourist industry stole it.

Julia had panicked. Harry was almost at the summit. He turned and waved and she heard his strong voice against the wind shouting, 'Am I in heaven, Granny?'

'No,' she replied and instantly regretted the word for in his eyes he was and it might be the only heaven he would ever know.

He raced back down to her, his body out of control, his arms outstretched. 'I'm going to fly, Granny, like the swallows.' He almost knocked her over, sending her stick flying, his arms around her, hugging her too hard, squeezing the breath out of her. How she loved that child. His arrival had been so unexpected and he was still out there somewhere, asking the same questions; his last text message had been from somewhere in the Middle East.

Two decades before Harry's birth, Julia had put in a lot of effort trying to find a suitable husband for his mother, Anna, whose good looks as she approached midlife were running out of time. The little lunch parties Julia had given for mothers with eligible sons hadn't worked. When Anna discovered that the sons drove Porsches and wore black leather designer jackets, she disliked them before she met them. So when the phone rang, Julia was taken off guard.

'Mum. I'm getting married on Tuesday at Hexham registry office. Any chance of you popping over to be a witness?'

Julia's first reaction to this news was to question whether mothers or any relatives were allowed to be witnesses. She would have to ring the registrar's office to be reassured. Selfishly, she also felt immediate relief that no flashy wedding was planned for she had never been up to, nor capable of, organising a social shindig where she needed to dress up and be exposed, however minor her role might be.

Still holding the phone, and anxious not to say the wrong thing or put a spanner in the works, she replied, 'How lovely, darling. Tell me about him. Do we know him?'

'No, Mother, you do not.'

She should have been able to trust her daughter; Anna was, after all, forty-three and had experienced things in her life that Julia had only dreamt about in hers. A gap year spent in Australia on a Queensland cattle station, rounding up cattle by helicopter and shooting feral bulls from the cockpit; sailing down the Amazon with natives.

Anna had eventually arrived home with a large lump on her skull and persistent throbbing in her head and Julia had insisted she visit the School of Tropical Medicine to have it looked at. The larvae of some obscure bug was busy hatching in her head, lodged in her skull. Had it been left alone to complete its life cycle, the specialist told her, it would have found its own way out but would not have survived in the cold British climate. At the time Julia felt that the specialist's only concern was for the insect, whereas Anna was left with a scar along her hairline which had destroyed the pigmentation of her hair. She had a distinctive white patch above her right eye. Julia thought it rather endearing; Anna said it looked as though she were going prematurely grey.

Julia tried to extract more information. 'What does he do?'

'He's a farmer.'

'Where?'

The name of a farm was given, Green Syke. Then her daughter added, 'He's been married twice before.'

When Anna heard her mother's intake of breath, she

put down the phone.

Julia looked at the calendar. Tuesday: just four days to do some detective work. Was he a wife beater with a criminal record? She imagined the worst and remembered her father's modus operandi when her brothers had brought unsuitable girlfriends home. Julia recalled one woman called Ginger with bright red hair whom David had picked up at a railway station and proposed to within a week. Father rang the family solicitor, his fishing buddy and best friend, who initiated legal searches which produced the welcome news that Ginger was already married.

Perhaps these things could be picked up on the internet but, like many of her diminishing generation, Julia had been left behind and when faced with a computer screen hardly knew where to start. She held a firm conviction that if she clicked the wrong button the whole machine would disappear into the ether.

It was midday Friday. Her solicitor, whom she hardly knew, went home early on a Friday. Nevertheless, Julia rang her and the woman was helpful. She said she could certainly find out within an hour whether there was a criminal record.

'What is Anna's boyfriend's name?'

But of course Julia had no idea, only the knowledge that he had been married twice before and the name of his farm. Julia was impressed when her solicitor rang back within the hour and reported no criminal or insolvency problems. His name was Matt O'Brien; the solicitor suggested Julia put out feelers among the farming community.

This was a sensitive area, not something you could easily bring into conversation with neighbours; northern farmers

15

in particular are inclined to be sparing in their praise of other farmers. So Julia approached the auctioneer at the local livestock mart whose knowledge of his clients' credibility – domestically, financially and otherwise – was second to none.

He did not hesitate on hearing the name. 'Eccentric, slightly mad, accident-prone, but he hasn't an ounce of badness in him.'

She spread the Hexham Ordnance Survey Map 77 on the table and, with the help of her magnifying glass, managed to locate the name of the farm. It was on the border of Cumbria and Northumberland, within the old kingdoms of Rheged and Bernicia with their history of Border reivers; within the forest of Spadeadam which was now synonymous with low-flying tornado bombers which screamed along the Pennines and the Eden Valley, practising their low-bombing skills, destroying the peace on warm sunny days. Julia had noticed how the cattle and sheep hardly looked up because they had adapted to the noise; it was the tourists who flinched. Now the bombers were screeching over Iraq, Syria, and Afghanistan, their collateral damage unheard. Julia thought it was rather like putting down rat poison in the farm buildings: you killed the rats but just as easily it could be the neighbours' cats or an owl which picked up carrion.

The map showed a long lane leading up to a cluster of buildings. Julia made some notes and decided to get in the car the following day and take a look.

The phone rang early; phone calls before eight usually heralded family emergencies and she picked up the receiver in a state of conditioned anxiety, expecting a familiar voice in a state of panic.

This one she didn't recognise; it was female. 'Is that Mrs Hampton?'

Julia sensed hostility and hesitated slightly before saying yes.

'I thought you should know, before your daughter marries him, that Matt O'Brien killed his father.'

'Who is this?'

'I hope he's told you about his other wives.'

Evil was coming at Julia down the line and her body responded before her mind. Her blood stopped pumping; there was a tightness across her chest; her hands shook and large red globules started dripping from her nose. The voice continued. Julia could tell it was unhinged and tried to stop listening; she was not hearing the words now, just stupidly accepting and absorbing the vitriol and hatred. Then the phone went dead.

She had taken the call in her bedroom and sat down quickly on the edge of the bed, shaking uncontrollably, the blood from her nose gathering momentum. When the phone rang, she had been looking in her diary to check the week's commitments. Now it was open at the day's date, covered in blood.

Julia didn't normally record events in her diary, its use was to remind her of future commitments, but she recorded this call. Still shaking an hour later, she wrote over the now-dried blood: 'Truly frightening phone call at eight this morning, absolutely vitriolic and malicious. Someone has got it in for Anna.' She was pleased she had made the effort, for one day evidence might be needed.

Later that day, with the map on the car seat beside her,

Julia drove towards the farm. It must be somewhere along here on the left, she thought. Perhaps there would be one of those smart signs with a picture of a cow and the name of a famous dairy herd.

She felt she had gone too far and found a muddy field gateway in which to turn the car. Driving more slowly, looking to the right, she saw a large, rusting tin box half-hidden in the grass and the remains of a wooden door with the name of the farm painted in red. The paint had been too thin when it was applied and had run down.

Turning up the heavily potholed lane, Julia noticed the abundance of well-managed trees. Though the lane itself was difficult to navigate, the grass verges on either side had been planted with crocus, white and purple, as far as the eye could see; their flower heads were beginning to wither, sending messages to their bulbs to restore their energy for the following year. Out of the corner of her eye she thought she saw four or five traditional domed beehives. The house was not visible; the drive must be a long one.

She started to worry. To go any further would be foolhardy; if she met someone, she had no wish to explain her presence. There didn't appear to be anywhere to turn the car so she would have to reverse over all those potholes and, in the process, would probably damage the car's sump. She got out to have a look.

She could hear a vehicle nearby, coming from the direction of where she imagined the farmhouse might be. Before she had time to get back in the car, a quad bike came around the corner very fast. It was driven by a naked man with what appeared to be a tea cosy on his head, one of those striped hand-knitted ones with three

18

tassels on the top which won prizes in the industrial and horticultural sections of village agricultural shows. Class 87: hand-knitted tea cosy made out of remnants of wool.

He jammed on the brakes, dislodging the sheepdog riding pillion. It came towards her, its tail wagging, sniffing her intimately. She patted its head; it was one of the old strain of border collies with patches of tan in its black and white coat. The man called her off, 'That'll do, Jess.' He got off the bike and came towards her and apologised for the tea cosy on his head; he made not the slightest effort to disguise his nakedness but apologised for the tea cosy.

'Since I was a child, I've always felt the cold through my head. I just grabbed the nearest thing. I was about to have a bath but thought I'd better check a cow first in the bottom lonnin. She's thinking of calving.'

Julia noticed that he walked with a severe limp and his right leg appeared to be encased in a filthy old sack. He saw her looking at it. 'I fell off a roof a couple of days ago but discharged myself from hospital. It's a bit painful but it will mend. It had better. I'm getting married on Tuesday.' He held out his hand. 'I'm Matt. Were you looking for someone?'

Julia was at a disadvantage. She really shouldn't be there and if she told the truth it would appear that she was prying, so she decided upon a little white lie. Had she thought it through, she would have recognised that it could turn eventually into a big white lie. She said, 'I needed to spend a penny so just turned up the first lane I could.'

'Just pop up to the house, the back door is open. Second door on the left. If you'll excuse me, I must check the cow. She's one that's had trouble calving in the past.'

Julia could recognise immediately what Anna saw in this man and, perhaps for the first time, began to admire her daughter and regret her own decision to marry a socially acceptable person.

She remembered the classroom words forced into her to get her through some exam. These flashes of ancient memories were becoming more frequent as old age descended. Tennyson, was it Elaine and Lancelot? Julia remembered vividly Miss Greenwood, head of English, her huge corseted bosom settling itself down on the desk top. She was one of the multitude of spinsters denied a mate by the First World War and held a bitterness within her. '*For he who loves me must have a touch of earth.*' Discuss. Perhaps Anna had studied Tennyson but never mentioned it. Julia thought how education was wasted on the young; its true value was felt when it was too late.

In the eyes of the world, Julia had married up and it had proved to be a disaster. Had she run off with the blacksmith's son, on whom she had developed a crush at the age of sixteen when she took her Exmoor pony, Betty, to have her feet trimmed, she knew that she would have been a good deal happier. Once upon a time there were romantic poems written about this sort of social dilemma; now it was called 'marrying beneath you' and you had to be strong to deal with the fall out and rejection such a union might produce.

Julia wondered whether Anna had thought this marriage through. Wraggle- taggle gypsies were all very well in romantic ballads and songs:

'What care I for a goose-feather bed

With the sheets turned down so bravely, O!
For to-night I shall sleep in a cold open field,
Along with the wraggle-taggle gipsies, O.'

Remembering those lines, the tune came back to her
and she started humming. Anna was about to take that
step which Julia had lacked the courage to take. Middle
class was a minefield of improprieties; you were stuck in
the middle, not sure where you should be, aware that those
snobby upper-crusty folk were hanging on your every
vowel and word usage, making it impossible to be yourself
in case you let yourself down. Who, Julia wondered, had
made up these rules? It certainly wasn't the French, whom
the British had been inclined to blame for their own
deficiencies since Agincourt.

Anna was about to break those rules in a big way. Julia
was aware of the social pitfalls, exclusion and unhappiness
that might await her and felt proud of her daughter. She
said thank you to Tennyson, at the same time wishing that
she had read Classics at university instead of becoming a
secretary and marrying Hugh.

She drove further up the lane, the potholes worsening.
She saw the house but couldn't get near it; ducks and hens
restricted her path and she was scared she might run over
one and squash it. She got out of the car and walked.

The back door was indeed open; mud, duck and hen
shit followed her into the house, it couldn't be avoided.
But when Julia lifted her eyes, she saw the most exquisite
paintings on the walls. They were everywhere. The house
itself appeared to be in a state of demolition and parts of
the outside walls were missing; her daughter may well have

to be prepared to live in 'a cold open field'. But on those walls which were still intact there hung beautiful, original watercolours of animals. One was of two hares, doing their mad March mating dance. Each hair was a single brush stroke; if Julia ran her cheek against it, she was certain she would feel a softness and if she blew on it the hairs would part, so delicately was it painted. It reminded Julia of the animal portraits by Ward Binks in the hall of her childhood home and she wondered what had happened to them.

She found the loo and returned to the car. Matt had returned, still naked, and was holding three goslings in his hands. He held them out for her to see and said, 'Aren't they beautiful?' She sensed the wonderment and awe in his voice.

Julia touched the soft grey down and marvelled at the beauty of their grotesqueness; they were so curiously put together, balancing on their yellow webbed feet. He held them up for her to have a closer look and it was then she saw his hands. They were not normal hands, they were the implements of toil: filthy, cankered, rough and huge. The goslings sensed the sensitivity in them and made no effort to escape.

His hands were in the position of a supplicant waiting to receive the Eucharist, one hand above the other as Julia had been taught to do in confirmation classes seventy years earlier in readiness for her first communion by the bishop of St Asaph. Then it had not meant a thing, but now it did.

Perhaps Matt was the new Adam? A tea cosy in place of a fig leaf?

CHAPTER 3

Julia's days had taken on a new dimension. They ran out of time more rapidly, governed by the mundane physical essentials of bathing, dressing and cooking, leaving her mind little space. Her body let her down by being too tired to do the things she wanted to do, to read again those half-read book before glaucoma took complete control.

She recalled that day, two decades ago, when Anna and Matt had become man and wife in the eyes of the law.

Julia had opened a door on which was written 'Registrar' and entered a small, deserted, unwelcoming waiting room with plain Victorian chairs pressed hard against the walls, horse hair escaping from splits in their black leather seats. A sign on the wall said 'Please wait here' and a large wall clock ticked its way to ten o'clock.

Anna had said ten o'clock but nothing else. Anna was never one for being on time and achieved a great deal by living by the seat of her pants, as the saying goes. Julia, who for the whole of her life felt she had never got anything right, decided that she had either got the date wrong, or the place, or both. Lessons learnt early were still ingrained in her mind; she had been taught as a child that being on time was good manners. She had always been too early for everything and wasted a good deal of time hanging around for others.

The minute hand on the clock crept passed twelve and she decided to wait until it reached the quarter hour. At ten past, the public door opened and a man of about fifty with greying hair sat down opposite her on the other side of the room. He looked ill at ease; he bent forward, elbows on his knees, his head down, his cement-encrusted overalls bearing a reddish tinge. Although he wasn't actually wringing his hands, Julia felt he was using them to comfort one another as though they were unhappy to find their owner's body in that position, wanting to be elsewhere where they could do more good.

After a few moments Julia thought she should pass the time of day. She made a comment about the weather to which he replied, 'Eye, fair clashy,' in local dialect.

Julia gave it another minute and tried again. 'Are you by any chance anything to do with Matt and Anna?'

'I've come as a witness.'

'I'm Anna's mother.'

Julia's breaking of the ice initiated a response. 'I've met your daughter once or twice.' Julia wondered where. 'Matt's had a bad life up to now. I hope Anna will sort him. Have you met his sister, Carla? She was responsible for the other two leaving.'

All this was far removed from what was expected and there was no way that any of it could be interpreted and printed in the social engagements page in the *Telegraph*.

The door of the inner office opened. A rather austere woman came out and enquired, 'Are you part of the O'Brien–Hampton wedding?'

Julia didn't feel part of anything. Perhaps she and the

man had been mistaken for the bride and groom.

There were voices and the outer door opened. Matt came in, dressed in jeans, open-necked checked shirt and sports jacket. His eyes told her that he recognised her immediately but he said nothing. This was all getting off on the wrong foot; Julia's intention to explain their last meeting as pure coincidence would sound hollow so she kept quiet.

Anna arrived at 10.20. 'Sorry, couldn't find a parking space. Hi, Mum, you found it OK? I see you've met Matt's friend Gary.' She was wearing an old pair of jeans and a hacking jacket; Julia remembered she had kept it from her Pony Club days and it was now far too small.

The registrar broke the tension. 'Normally when parties arrive late we turn them away but today, as there isn't another couple to follow, I shall make an exception.'

They were ushered into a pleasant room with comfortable modern chairs in rows to welcome well-wishers, of whom there were none. Hugh had refused to come to anything which, in his eyes, was not done properly. On the registrar's desk was a small bowl of imitation anemones, the colours garish and false. She sensed Matt's disapproval of them.

As witnesses, she and Gary were seated together. Their introduction had been perfunctory and neither knew what was expected of them.

Julia hadn't had a chance to say a word to Anna. Matt was smiling with his arm around her, his huge gnarled-leather hand across her chest. His presence filled the room; Julia wished she had married someone like that and hoped Anna would appreciate him.

It was over in fifteen minutes. Julia listened to the

registrar's words – they all sounded remarkably sensible. There was nothing about worldly goods or procreation. She signed something as requested alongside Gary, who took his time with laborious concentration. He had left writing behind him when he left school at fourteen.

Anna said, 'We've got to dash, there's a couple of cows calving.'

Matt came up to Julia, smiling, gave her a hug and said, 'Nice to meet you again.' He never questioned nor saw suspicion in their first meeting and ignored her mendacity.

The simplicity of the civil ceremony had impressed Julia. In the eyes of the law, Matt and Anna were now husband and wife but she felt a conviction that what was needed – by her but probably not by them – was a spiritual dimension to their union.

Other than being present at weddings and funerals, Julia had not been inside a church for a while. She had become a stranger to prayer, her faith flimsy, unsure that God was still there or anywhere. She had had a near encounter with death fifteen years earlier, which could have proved His existence once and for all, but someone had rescued her and she had been denied reaching the pearly gates and testing their authenticity.

Lately, on rising and before dressing, she had got into the habit of opening the back door, standing on the weathered, moss-encrusted sandstone step, its shape hollowed by feet from the past, and trying to make contact with Him again. She wanted to greet Him – 'Hi God, how are you today?' – to regain that lost sense of certainty and awe. She wanted to see Heaven as she had as a child, up there somewhere in the clouds.

She recalled the sandstone steps of her youth, scrubbed pristine daily by Marjorie the kitchen maid at the tradesmen's entrance at the back of the house. Marjorie's raw red hands wringing out dirty cloths, her muscled, masculine arms rejuvenating the pinky-red of the steps with the rudding stone, the tradition and duty of house-proud northern women from another age. Was it sandstone dust on Gary's overalls? Sandstone, she thought, so like people: hard on the outside but porous and fragile inside, disintegrating when the elements got to it.

The clouds were the same clouds of her youth: cirrus, their wispy, ephemeral, presence auguring a fine day. Their presence high in the sky might nowadays be mistaken for the profligate vapour trail of an international jumbo jet. The low-slung nimbus, their mother-of-pearl and steel greys fusing, were heavily laden with rain. They rested for a short while on the fell tops, then were blown by a sharp east wind before releasing their cargo, the wet coldness slapping her face to restore her from a sleepless night.

Sometimes the leafless winter silhouette of the damson tree outside the kitchen window was bent double by the easterly wind. It had been planted – or seeded itself – in the wrong place a century ago and was too exposed to bear fruit. It was whipped by the wind into barrenness, its branches like the clouds rearranged by the wind into shapes. Today the top branches looked like Neptune's tripod or perhaps Satan's fork.

Julia had surprised herself by her decision to start dipping her toes in the sea of faith again and wasn't at all sure why. It may have been that the Christian faith was having a bad time, had its back to the wall, and now that it appeared to be the underdog she felt it her duty to defend it. Perhaps she needed to be certain that her payments were up to date, the final premium, that last instalment paid before payback day arrived. Perhaps it was a longing for a return to the cosy, safe, nostalgic childhood of a privileged upbringing. On her bedroom wall she still had a religious painting by Margaret Tarrant, Jesus within a tryptic with a wood in the background, surrounded by animals, the caption in gold lettering: 'All Creatures Great and Small'.

Julia avoided going to church on Sundays when people were still a little inclined to dress up. Now the vicar had abandoned the Common Book of Prayer of her youth and announced, 'You will find the next prayer on pamphlet so-and-so.' He called out the numbers like ecclesiastical bingo and the congregation shuffled to find the correct piece of paper, their concentration diverted. Although Julia had enjoyed a good singalong at Morning Prayer in the past, somehow the hymn lyrics had become detached from the expectations of the twenty-first century.

Instead, she started going to a small gathering on Thursdays mornings, a quick half hour of readings, prayers, Eucharist, coffee and chat. One line of prayer had touched a nerve: 'When we were still far off, your Son met us and brought us home.' It seemed relevant, a quick satisfying recharging of faith for the mainly elderly, good-natured ladies in anoraks. There she met a delightful smiley old man who she thought was a retired bishop because he occasionally helped with the Eucharist but turned out not to be. Julia privately christened his wife Mrs Proudie because she reminded her of the character in Trollope's *Barchester Chronicles*.

Julia tried to avoid the days when she knew Mrs Proudie would be there. It wasn't that she disliked her; in fact, she admired her greatly. Mrs Proudie was outgoing, a characteristic Julia tried to emulate, although when Julia tried it felt she was being pushy. On occasion, Mrs Proudie being outgoing could turn into her being overbearing and she was inclined to usurp people's personal space. Once, when Julia and she had met by chance in the supermarket, her enthusiastic greeting had driven Julia backwards into a stack of baked beans and they had crashed to the floor. Also, Mrs Proudie was always immaculately dressed: earrings, jewellery at ten in the morning. Julia found it difficult to find a clean Barbour in her rush to be early.

The Thursday after Matt and Anna's civil ceremony, Julia decided she would go and say a little prayer for the newly married couple. She must have misheard Mrs Proudie at their last meeting – hadn't she said would be in South Africa visiting her married daughter? Just as the service started, Mrs Proudie came in and sat in the pew in front, bringing the congregation up to nine. Julia noted that she was wearing a sort of furry confection around her neck and wondered whether it was real leopard. No, the spots were too big; perhaps it was ocelot.

During the Peace, when everyone had to say 'Peace be with you' and hug everyone else, Mrs Proudie turned round, clasped Julia's hand and gave her a kiss on the cheek. The ocelot hairs tickled her cheek and smelled of naphthalene; the fur must be real.

Julia heard the whispered words: 'It must be awful for you, Anna marrying that man. Very distressing. I feel for you.' And as an afterthought, as Mrs Proudie turned away, she said, 'Peace be with you'.

Chapter 4

Harry had arrived promptly, nine months after the wedding. Anna had opted not to know the sex of the child she was carrying; she preferred surprises.

From the moment of introduction, that first glimmer of recognition, Harry and Julia had hit it off. They were connected, earthed by a mutual understanding, fuses blown by the same faults. At ten months old, he snatched at her pearls, the real ones worth a fortune, which had once belonged to her grandmother. Their knotted string, grown weak by age, broke under Harry's determined hand and the pearls scattered on the wooden floor in a silver hailstorm of noise, some bouncing and disappearing between ill-fitting floorboards. Julia and Harry both laughed.

For Anna, Harry's gestation had been uneasy for she didn't really want him. She was not maternal unless she was delivering the young of animals. She had foreseen difficulties and been brave enough to say to cooing friends that she would find motherhood hard but, as always when something inevitable came into her life uninvited, she made the best of it, dealt with it, determined to do right. She decided to breastfeed Harry for as long as possible.

Anna succumbed to mastitis sooner than most but was determined to keep going for Harry's sake, for that is what all the expensive books she had purchased prior to his birth had told her to do. She knew all about mastitis; having been brought up on a farm she had treated it in sheep many times and recognised it early by the sheep's stiff gait and hard, swollen, purpling udder which had ceased its flow of milk. Unless you gave the animal a good dose of antibiotics, the udder became gangrenous and fell off and the sheep died. Anna wasn't going to allow that to happen to her. Her GP was liberal in his supply of antibiotics and Harry eventually took the matter into his own hands. At eight months old, when offered the engorged swollen breast, he pushed it away.

After his birth Julia had, because she felt she had recently rediscovered God, tentatively enquired about a christening. Had they godparents in mind? Had Matt any suitable relatives or friends?

'Hasn't Matt got a sister?' She asked the question in an underhand way, already knowing the answer, trying to find out more. Her own values of family solidarity were instinctive. She and Hugh had not sought godparents for their children outside the clan, believing that families should stick together and not seek out influential wealthy acquaintances who might give a godchild a leg up later in life but be a bit of a dead loss when it came to spiritual mentoring.

'Yes, Carla,' Anna replied. 'But they don't get on.'

'Where does she live?'

'About a mile away. She married an unpleasant property developer called Theo. Matt says he's a bully and beats her up. They have a teenage son, Piers. I've never met her. Matt says she's trouble, always seeking attention.'

So for the time being the matter of Harry's christening was shelved, to be dealt with later. Later turned out to be seven years when, at a family birthday gathering, someone had asked him, 'Well, young man, what are you going to do with your life?'

Harry had replied without hesitation, 'I'm going to be baptised.'

There was a pause in the conversation but Matt took control. Julia was grateful that he had, for her family still thought of him as a bit of a gypsy and had only accepted him because of his good humour. He put his huge arm around his son's shoulder and asked, 'Why?'

And then Harry, who was beginning to feel that his parents were mildly dysfunctional, took matters into his own hands. 'Because I want to be part of God's family. And I want to choose my own godparents.'

Julia thought no one could really argue with that, unless you were Richard Dawkins and saw the possibility of a money-making book in the remark. She wondered how you went about christening an eight year old; did he have to be submerged in water like John the Baptist? Julia told herself to stop worrying; people didn't have to wear hats at christenings nowadays unless they were Kate Middleton or a footballer's wife.

It was Matt who arranged for a quiet ten-minute ceremony after Matins at St Oswalds the following Sunday. There was a last-minute hitch because Harry was too small to bend over the font but Matt, without asking the vicar, went into the vestry and returned with four telephone directories for the child to climb on.

Harry already knew that his father did things without

making a fuss. Matt had a quiet detachment, was totally oblivious to the censure of others and, if challenged, laughed it off. Harry had inherited those traits and, by watching his father, he had learnt very early on that whining got you nowhere. Nothing in life really mattered and he accepted his father's eccentricities without embarrassment, understanding that a moral establishment was far more important than laws passed to placate a vociferous minority.

There had been that incident at the school sports day when Harry had been picked to represent his house in the relay race. Anna had a dentist's appointment that afternoon and couldn't make it. She said to Matt, 'Do go and support him – it would mean so much to him to have you there.'

But of course Matt set little value on an enforced education; it was not what he wished for his son. He would rather have him nearby each day and teach him how to farm and care for livestock. He said, 'I have to collect a few stirks that afternoon. If I remember, I'll pop in.'

As he possessed neither watch nor mobile, time meant nothing to him and it was only when he was returning home with the load of cattle that he remembered. Still wearing his working clothes, a tattered Barbour, jeans full of holes, a woolly hat and welly boots covered in cow muck, his hands unwashed, he parked the Land Rover and trailer alongside the BMWs and stood at the back of the cheering crowd.

The stirks, thinking they were back home on the farm, started mooing as cattle do in order to make contact again with friends and relatives. The sound was magnified by the metal sides of their container.

Harry heard them and knew Matt was there. As the

baton was passed to him he ran faster than he had ever done in his life and his team won.

When Harry related all this to Julia later, she asked him, 'Was it a bit of an embarrassment Dad turning up like that?'

Harry replied, 'I would have been far more embarrassed if he had turned up in a Rolls Royce.'

Although his father didn't understand him, Harry understood his father. He knew his father would have liked a quiver full of children but his mother had put a stop to that. Harry, aware that he would always be an only child and that there were deficiencies in his upbringing, chose his godparents with care and wisdom to fit in with his present predicament of feeling he was the parent to his mother and father.

His choices had been honoured. One of his godfathers was his eldest cousin, twenty years his senior, who Harry looked up to because he had stood up to the education system and dropped out of university to become an apprentice engineer in the Nissan factory in Sunderland. He was now self-employed, could find work by just snapping his fingers and was making a fortune. Harry's other godfather was Gary, Dad's best man, who would mend his bike when Dad was too busy painting pictures and looking after the animals.

There were raised eyebrows when Harry chose Chloe, the pretty smiling waitress at MacDonald's who was working her way through drama school, as his godmother. Harry had an intuitive gift and recognised instantly the real value of people; he had fallen in love with her. She hugged him, which his mother rarely did, and asked, 'How's my favourite boyfriend?' He noticed how everyone liked her.

Julia had to admit that Chloe was a delight. She was like a marshmallow, her skin perfect, soft and scented; she had kept her puppy fat into her late twenties. Her voice was calm and gentle and her thoughts for others were considerate and worldly wise. Her long black hair had streaks of pink and her doe eyes were accentuated by cleverly applied mascara and eye shadow, giving her a kind of Amy Whitehouse look. Julia sensed in her a vulnerable softness waiting to be savaged by a hostile world.

Harry had written a note to each of the prospective godparents on a piece of paper from his Star Wars writing set with a picture of Darth Vader, the evil one, printed in the corner. All three recipients had accepted his invitation and stood with him, making promises that they fully intended to keep.

That was how Chloe became part of Julia's extended family, for the girl didn't appear to have anyone of her own. No one knew where she had come from or whether she had family; she never mentioned them, although they sensed there was a boyfriend in the background. Her accent was mild Geordie and it was assumed that she was a product of the north east. In her youth she might have been one of those hardy Newcastle lasses disgorged half naked from pubs on a Friday night. She was streetwise and, like Matt, she was able to deal with life. At the time of the christening, she told Julia that she was hoping to get together with three colleagues and perform in the Fringe at the Edinburgh Festival but it was difficult to get a slot.

Harry's ability to think for himself had come at a very early age. He was his own man by the age of three when he had his first brush with authority. It was unfortunate that the principal of his pre-nursery school was called Miss Kelly. At three years old, Harry was discovering the deliciousness of onomatopoeic words: *jelly* and *belly*, words to be mixed like poster paints to create different sound colours. Changing the first letter of *hunt* and *punt* to a *c* and trying an *f* before *muck*, *puck* and *suck* to see which letter painted the best picture was fun – until other children followed his lead and parents complained that he was corrupting their toddlers. Anna was asked to take him away.

Years later, when Anna recounted this episode to Chloe at Harry's christening, Chloe said, 'You were well rid of that school. Harry had a narrow escape from tight-arsed teachers lacking in imagination who should have recognised and rejoiced in such experimentation. Shakespeare would surely have approved.'

Julia was unsure what tight-arsed meant; it had yet to become part of her vocabulary but she felt that her beloved old England was becoming just that. It had lost its sense of humour and when anyone had a slip of the tongue, reciting a nursery rhyme learnt at their mother's knee and inadvertently letting slip a word deemed offensive, there was a great deal of huffing and puffing which attracted media attention, fanning the flames of misunderstanding and intolerance and demands for apologies for nothing important.

Harry saw all this; by the age of six he had noticed this strange and unreasonable behaviour in adults, the double standards of what you could or could not say. 'Granny, do I really have to say that when it isn't true?' he had asked her.

He was quickly learning the complexity and contradictions in the words 'freedom of speech', that a freedom to say something offensive to others was not a freedom worth having. And that a freedom not to be able to say something that might offend others was not worth having.

His awareness of this had come to a head in his first term at primary school at the weekly swimming lesson at the local baths. The first Julia heard about it was a phone call late at night from Anna. The high-pitched tone of her voice heralded disaster. 'Harry is being threatened with exclusion from school. It will go on his CV and ruin his whole life.'

In Julia's day it was called 'being expelled'. She did not like the word 'exclusion'; it was a hurtful word, an 'I don't want to play with you but if you come up to adult expectations, we may let you back in the game' word. Julia preferred expelled, a positive word; you knew where you were and could adjust to the situation.

It was difficult to find out exactly what had happened. Experience had taught her to believe Harry rather than the school or his parents.

'But, Granny, all I was doing was looking at people's feet.' Drying himself off after showering, Harry had wandered into the female changing room. The cubicle doors did not extend to the floor and a gap of six inches, which allowed water to drain into a small channel, invited inquisitive young eyes. Harry was discovered crawling along the wet floor, looking underneath each door.

'Perverted, inappropriate behaviour,' the school said.

Anna appeared to be hysterical. Julia had written a

rambling, not very accurate but placatory letter to the school which had cooled the situation.

So it was that she got into the habit of defending Harry, rightly or wrongly, against all odds. She saw, as he did, that there were deficiencies in his upbringing. Once upon a time she had believed in her own principles but life had made her doubt herself. Now she believed that God was allowing her a little longer to keep an eye on Harry and to try and sort herself out.

When secondary education was no longer in the future but beckoning a couple of months away, Harry's school reports arrived with their monotonous nag of 'could do better'. 'Everyone in the world could do better. Why pick on me?' he protested.

Julia, seeing his frustration, came to his rescue; she got on Facebook so that they could exchange thoughts. At eighty-five, she found it a bit of a challenge. She was not computer literate; she owned a computer but it felt like an unwelcome guest in her house, demanding a cordon bleu meal when she could only serve up fish and chips. It had belonged to Hugh and since his death she had written a novel on it, bravely sent a few emails and tried to use the Internet but she could never find the links she was being instructed to click on and felt the machine was working against her. It was like the Rubik cube an optimistic grandchild had given her for Christmas to keep her mind healthy in its dotage; all it did was add to her lifelong belief in her own stupidity.

She knew that she wasn't alone in her frustration. Had not Charles Lamb, so tedious at school, vented his frustration three centuries ago and proclaimed: 'In everything which relates to science I am a whole Encyclopaedia behind the rest of the world'? Her heart went out to him. He had also said something rather uncomplimentary about the Scots which made Julia warm to him even more. It was not that Julia disliked the Scots – they were her near neighbours – but they had become in thrall to a bossy, vindictive head girl.

She made an appointment with a lovely lady called Pam at the local library to take her through the IT equivalent of 'C is for cat' and under Pam's patient tuition Julia quickly picked up the skills she needed. Now she could talk to Harry on Facebook.

Harry, free of parental interference and knowing that his secrets were safe with his grandmother, let his thoughts off the leash. He always ended his messages with lots of little sun-coloured smiley faces, twenty rows of kisses and the statement: *Granny, I love you more as each week goes by.*

So when he sent a message saying: *Granny, Mum and the school are trying to imprison my mind. I have to be monitored at all times because my thoughts don't coincide with theirs. I feel like a convict. Dad shouts a bit when I won't help on the farm but he's OK*, Julia saw it as a personal challenge.

Having been shown the exterior of the grammar school Anna and his primary school headmistress had in mind, the Holy Grail and the sole topic of mealtime conversations within the homes of pushy parents, Harry announced, 'It looks like Colditz.' His grandfather Hugh had told Harry all about Colditz, shown him photos of Harry's great-uncle's imprisonment within its impenetrable walls during the Second World War. 'I'm not going there,' Harry protested and refused to sit for the entrance examination though his teachers had told Anna and Matt that he would sail through.

Julia's own mother, in her day, had called this kind of dissent as being 'agin' the government. In the 1930s being 'agin' something was different from being 'agin' anything in 2016. Then it was applauded, revered, accepted as British eccentricity. Stroppiness made people smile; it was what made us Brits great. But now the word 'different' had been expunged from everyday vocabulary. The twenty-first century was not turning out to be the enlightened one all those expensive fireworks at the Millennium had promised.

The phone rang: Anna. 'Don't you dare interfere, Mother. I don't like the way Harry confides in you. He won't talk to me or Matt.'

It was round about that time, eleven-plus time, that Chloe announced she and her long-term Rastafarian partner were getting married. The nuptials were enormous fun. Chloe had faith and she enlisted the help of her local Methodist preacher to make the ceremony a real celebration. It was themed but not in a conventional way; *Life, Love and Laughter* it said on the programme that was roughly printed and run off on a friend's computer. The wedding dress did not cost a fortune; Chloe had confided in Julia later on, when they knew one another really well, 'I got it at Oxfam.'

Julia was chauffeured to the wedding by Matt and Anna, together with young Harry. As always with anything connected to Matt and Anna, they were hopelessly late and crept in at the back but then were ushered to the front. Harry had been given the responsibility of reading a poem

41

by W.H. Auden, which was given to him as he walked through the door.

People were laughing and it was only when the four of them sat down, the tension of their late arrival subsiding, that they saw what people were laughing at. A huge screen showing a silent movie from the 1920s was flickering black-and-white images above the altar. Harold Lloyd was hanging onto the back of a tram car.

Julia looked more carefully at the programme. On it was written quite clearly: 'Get me to the church on time.'

Anna was fretting at Harry being put under pressure by the reading but he rose to the occasion with his usual self-assurance, as Julia had known he would. He recited 'O tell me the truth about love' with perfect diction, pausing at the right times and looking the congregation straight in the eye without the hint of a snigger, for he understood the honesty and beauty in the words.

'When it comes, will it come without warning
Just as I'm picking my nose.'

Later he said, 'Is that really poetry, Granny? It's good stuff, better than boring old prose. I love the density of the words.'

Julia had thought what excellent judgement Harry had exhibited when he had chosen Chloe as his godmother.

The disco in the evening in the basement of the local arts centre in the middle of Newcastle was noisy and tiring and Julia dreaded the long walk back to the car park by the church. Harry took her arm to guide her across the street. The Saturday nightclubs were spewing out their revellers onto the pavements, the *thud thud thud* of music making the city vibrate. The second Earl Grey looked down from his pedestal at the top of Grainger Street, having seen it all before. Now half-dressed girls sprawled, spewing the contents of their stomachs onto the pavements, unknowingly surrendering their sacred virginity in a piss-splashed doorway, replacing the ragged, drink-sodden poor of Grey's day, trailing their children around the hostelries for a pennyworth of gin.

Julia felt a sadness for those young girls but at the same time admired them. Their semi-nakedness defied the freezing cold night and they were so pretty and self-assured, which made Julia question why they felt the need to get plastered at weekends. But of course it was for the same reason that she had that secret litre bottle of Grouse hidden behind a giant bottle of tomato sauce in the kitchen cupboard – a pleasurable way to escape the expectations of society. And Julia suspected that they, just like she, hadn't a clue who or what society was.

She removed her hat. She had been the only person wearing one and it made her look conspicuous but she was conditioned. It was her only hat and well known at weddings; slightly too big, it gently changed its position on her head from time to time. She quite enjoyed putting it on as a form of fancy dress to become someone else. Pale lilac, large brimmed, with feathers and twiddly bits, it suited her.

Harry said, 'I'll carry your hat for you, Granny,' and put it on his head.

As they passed a bar, a man in a pink tutu stood in front of Harry simulating a sex act. Harry asked, 'Is that a gay bar, Granny? Why do they behave like that?'

She found it difficult to answer and be truthful. She wanted him to retain his innocence for a little longer but

43

she already knew it was too late – the media had made certain that innocence was a dirty word.

'Yes, it is a gay bar and they behave like that because they are trying to find a kind of happiness.' She knew Harry was mentally questioning her reply. She added quickly in order to divert the subject, 'Aren't we lucky to have such a loving family?'

He pressed her elbow more tightly to his side. 'It is you, Granny, who hold us all together.'

How like her favourite brother Jack, long-since dead, Harry was becoming. Almost a century divided their lives but Jack's make up was in Harry's DNA; Harry was also Matt's son, so he carried a double whammy of dissenting and sanguine genes which the less loving of the human race found annoying. Both Matt and Harry found it easy to laugh off things when blame was all around them, but Julia had witnessed in them a line that they were unprepared to cross when injustice affected others. At times their anger exploded like the wrath of God when He had tired of being a loving forgiving God and sent a few floods, earthquakes, doses of pestilence and famine to give mankind a warning. At times Julia thought Matt and Harry could do with a course in anger management; she had heard about such things.

Once, while watching *Columbo*, her favourite programme because you knew who the murderer was right at the beginning, she had fallen asleep and woken to a programme about anti-social behaviour. Some ineffective young woman with a degree in psychology was yattering on about anger management to a truculent teenager with a ring through his nose. Julia, cross that she had allowed herself to miss the end of *Columbo*, shouted at the TV, 'For God's sake, just give him a pile of old plates to smash.'

She recalled her mother doing that when she was angry with father; Mother kept a pile of crockery she disliked especially for the purpose. Julia sometimes wondered, when watching *Flog It!*, how many pieces of Clarice Cliff and Susie Potter had bitten the dust to assuage her mother's temper.

Julia instinctively knew that, in trying to protect the truth, one day Harry would run into trouble. She had to reassure him that when this happened she was there for him, but she feared he was beginning to doubt her ability to do so. Her dependence on a walking stick, her third leg as Harry called it, wouldn't look good in a court of law.

Chapter 5

Julia couldn't remember the exact date when the real trouble started. It must have been when Harry was about eighteen months old because she recalled Anna saying that he was still in his high-sided cot. Anna had mentioned one or two strange happenings: farm gates left open so that stock strayed and the police were called; the oil tank tampered with; water in the quad bikes' fuel tanks. She said she had the feeling that they were being watched.

At two in the morning, there was banging on the farmhouse door. Matt, a heavy sleeper, half conscious only when he knew a cow might calve in the night and his mind was on standby, didn't hear it. The banging became more frantic and Anna, barefoot, went downstairs, switched on the outside light and opened the door. Standing on the step was a woman aged about fifty. Anna noticed the expensive satin negligée shimmering seductively in the yard light; there were splashes of blood on it. Lifting her eyes to the woman's face, she saw yesterday's mascara mingling with tears and blood from a head wound above a swollen eye.

The woman was weeping hysterically. 'Please help me,' her voice slurred.

Although they had never met, Anna knew this was Carla. The heavy makeup over a lined, sun-bed tanned face told her so and, beneath the swollen cheeks, Carla shared the same impressive bone structure as Matt. She had long red fingernails and wrists that still wore their daytime bling; the hem of her nightdress was wet from the night's dew and farmyard muck and mud covered her bare feet. She must have run across the fields.

Anna said, 'Quickly, come in out of the cold. I'll fetch a blanket and make a hot drink.'

'Oh thank you, thank you. May I stay with you overnight?'

'Of course.' Anna had had many experiences but had never before been in the position to offer real sanctuary. She unfolded a blanket and put it around Carla's cold, shaking shoulders.

'You'd better not tell Matt I'm here,' Carla said.

But it was too late for the commotion had woken Harry. He was standing up in his cot, the beam from the landing light shining through the open door into his smiling face; he looked like one of those cherubs Michelangelo cleverly painted upside down on the ceiling in the Sistine chapel ceiling.

Carla may have seen her redemption in him, for she rushed towards him and shouted, 'What a lovely, lovely little boy,' and plucked him out of the cot. His cries aroused Matt, who misunderstood and saw nothing other than his son in the unstable arms of his sister.

'Put my son down. Don't ever touch him again,' he barked.

When she heard this story from Anna over the phone, Julia felt ill. She didn't really want to know, but that was before she had looked up the word 'allegory'.

'There was an awful row,' Anna continued. 'But I insisted

that Carla be offered sanctuary and Matt eventually agreed.'

'Is she still with you?'

'No, she left of her own volition. It must have been about five o'clock because we didn't hear her go. Matt was up by five to check the livestock and found the bed empty, so I phoned around eight to make certain she was safely home and ask whether I could help in any way. She talked as though nothing had happened. She told me to leave her alone and said she especially didn't want my help.'

Julia kept her anxieties to herself; she was unsure of herself but she possessed one certainty – her instinct. She had never mentioned to Anna that malicious, early-morning telephone call before the wedding. She also suspected that Matt had never mentioned his first meeting with his future mother-in-law, his intuition telling him why and his wisdom telling him to keep quiet.

Julia hadn't realised when the malicious calls started in earnest. The phone went five or six times in the middle of the night and no one answered when she replied. She imagined they were being made by cold callers in Mumbai trying to sell her something.

At first she always tried to be polite to cold callers; she would ask their names and about their families until her efforts to be friendly became too exhausting. She recalled an exchange with a charming man from Mumbai. She had asked his name.

'Omish.'

Julia misheard, confused his name with Amish, and subjected him to a monologue of how she admired the Amish people.

Omish, if that really was his name, listened patiently

for five minutes and then replied with immense courtesy, 'Dear, dear lady, what an interesting person you are. I would love to spend the morning talking with you, you remind me of my mother. But sadly I am not permitted to use up more of your precious time otherwise I shall lose my job and I have a wife and five children to support.'

Julia asked, 'What are the names of your children?' and the phone went dead.

Now calls were coming at all times of the day and night and there was never anyone on the other end of the line. Every time the phone rang she jumped. She suspected who it was but had no proof. She could install one of those phones which tell you who is on the other end but this was yet more technology to try and understand as well as extra expense. Her imagination was taking hold and she wished it would go away; she demanded that her fears leave her alone but her mind wouldn't obey.

Eventually Julia confided in Anna and found that her daughter and Matt were receiving similar calls. And in the middle of all that, there was Harry to protect.

Chapter 6

There were no witnesses to the incident. It was midday and Harry was at school, his first term at the local comprehensive. Anna was in town doing the Tesco run. She returned to find a police car in the farmyard with its lights flashing, the back door wide open and voices in the house. The kitchen phone was dangling impotent, a dead weight at the end of its cord.

Two policemen were taking notes, their presence threatening. They were young bobbies, menacing, dressed in readiness for a tough night in the city, technology tucked into their belts: walkie-talkie, truncheon, laser gun, pepper spray.

Matt was sitting down, visibly shaken; as Anna said later, 'It takes a lot to shake Matt.'

Julia instinctively knew that the police would not take the matter seriously for Matt's eccentricity was well known and his local reputation for having reivers' blood in his veins had gone before him. His mother was an Armstrong and that streak of wildness, cussedness and independence had been gossiped about for decades. His heritage raced ahead of him to rise up and ambush him from time to time.

'Do you honestly think your brother-in-law and nephew would break into your house in broad daylight and threaten to beat you up? We know them as a couple of decent guys.'

Matt replied, 'Yes, and if you had not arrived in time they would have done it. They heard your car and ran off over the fields. I was phoning for you when they tried to break down the door. You can see the frame is splintered. I dropped the phone to close an open window downstairs, but they were through before I could stop them. They pinned me down and said "We've got you now, you bugger," and then they heard the police siren and scarpered. My 999 call will have been recorded at the station.'

But later, when Anna phoned the police station to ask them for a transcript of the phone call, its existence was denied. When Anna tried to discuss the incident, Matt said, 'Leave it,' and added, 'You won't get justice. My brother-in-law Theo and PC Mosscrop are members of the same Lodge. It's just jealousy. Theo and Carla can't bear the thought that we have produced a son a bit late in life.'

And Anna had left it. She had been unaware until that moment that Harry's birth could cause such hatred, that the farm and its five hundred acres, tied up in the will of Matt and Carla's grandfather, would no longer go to Carla's son but to Matt's.

Then, thinking she was doing the right thing, Julia had done the wrong thing. She told Anna about the decade-old malicious phone call. At the time she had kept quiet to protect Anna from what she had honestly believed to be local nastiness. Now things were falling into place and to fabricate in order to assuage another's distress was not a good policy.

Anna was furious. 'Why on earth didn't you tell us? Matt would have known it was Carla and we could have taken out an injunction or something.'

Julia remembered Harry's words: 'You hold us all together, Granny.' It was a lovely thought if it were true, but the burden was becoming too great. She was getting too old to take on the unhappiness and struggles of others. Although she could have dealt with it once upon a time, she now felt a great desire to relinquish the responsibility.

She felt that her life was becoming like the small circular magnet she kept in her untidy top drawer to keep her hairpins together. It attracted an assortment of other debris: clinging to it were hearing-aid batteries, drawing pins, paperclips, broken clasps from seldom-used jewellery. Her mind was attracting the broken remains and loose fragments of other people's lives.

Would the incident with Matt and his brother-in-law be reported in the local press? Julia was anxious; she abhorred publicity in any form. As they did so many times, Julia's thoughts drifted to Hugh. She had not bought a newspaper since he died. When he was alive, he enjoyed shouting at *The Times* and applauding Thunderer, putting his own spin on what others had written. She had never managed to get him interested in Sudoku, codeword or the easy crossword which she did while cooking lunch. They might have prevented his mind going the way it did at the end. At least he had been spared the trauma which was engulfing his younger daughter.

And now she was missing Hugh's blue badge. When he was with her, they could park the car anywhere to nip into a newsagent; buying a paper had now become a long drawn-out affair of trying to find a parking space, fumbling in her overloaded purse for the correct coins, dropping it and her stick, and having to go back to the car for her other specs.

She had been tempted to use the blue badge after Hugh died; she felt that her need was just as legitimate as his had been. But she had handed it in on his death as her generation did automatically. Honesty was part of their fibre, like truth. Truth now only became truth if it was in the interest of the person extolling it. Real truth, once taught universally, seemed to be struggling. Julia wondered if the classics were still taught in comprehensives. Would Harry ever hear about, God, Confucius, Socrates Plato Aristotle and Euripides?

That evening Julia Facebooked Harry, curious to know whether he had heard of Socrates. Having topped himself, the philosopher might have got a mention in *Horrible Histories*.

At school, do they teach you about Socrates who took hemlock?

No, Granny. This afternoon we had two sessions of sex education. What is hemlock, Granny? Love you lots and lots and lots and lots and lots and lots and lots, big hug, followed by twelve smiley yellow faces and four lines of kisses.

'Shit,' Julia thought and chickened out of the responsibility of trying to give an honest answer.

Her mind was orbiting again, absorbing things which eighty years ago could have been useful, perhaps got her into a university. Her thoughts churned away; maybe it was her responsibility to do something about it. Join the University of the Third Age, write articles, ring politicians, go to meetings and heckle, join marches, go on fun runs for a good cause.

But now it was her body which was not listening. She had always been astounded at the ability of her mind to control her body; now, when her mind was anxious, it sent messages of nausea and palpitations to her body. Her mind and body were incapable of synchronisation. If she bent down, she got vertigo; putting on her socks was a hazardous affair and she had brought into use a contraption which somehow had landed up in the box room after her mother died, a stick with a grab on the end where she could hook the sock onto her toe. Council road sweepers used them for picking up litter. She remembered that when Mother had used it, Julia had ridiculed her, thought she was posturing.

When she finally made it to the nearest town the local newspaper was sold out, adding to Julia's anxiety. Perhaps the incident at Matt and Anna's farm had been reported in headlines on the front page. Provincial journalists, weary of reporting flower shows and livestock prices, might have seen the chance of a scoop. Their readers, anxious for a neighbourhood scandal to enliven their lives, would have bought it in droves.

She bought *The Times* instead to read the letters' page to try and keep herself in touch with the thoughts of others, to reassure herself that there were still people out there attempting to reassert common sense. But human misery assailed her in every printed word: Ebola, ISIS, Ukraine, Sudan, Lydia, Syria, child abuse and more child abuse. Julia had been the recipient of child abuse in her youth but accepted it as part of growing up. It had, however, made her more determined to see only the good in people.

It was the same on television. It had become the platform from where a privileged few were licensed to be thoroughly unpleasant to others; trivial finger pointing, blame given to those whose beliefs and freedoms were given short shrift by clever anchor persons who probed, twisted and skewered dark memories from people. Lord Reith's vision was foundering, together with his reputation. Julia remembered some revered octogenarian elder statesman, whose name now escaped her but had once been an anchor in her life. In reply to the dragging up of an incident from his past, he had replied, 'Why did I do that? I don't know. The past is a different country; they did things differently there and I was twenty-one.'

That was exactly how Julia felt. You do things in life of which later you are made to feel ashamed. That was why the last five minutes of life were so important and forgiveness so vital, why the last rites of the Catholic Church became significant but were unappreciated until your time came. All that soothing Latin, incomprehensible at school, finally made sense, became real, rather like a scene in a Miss Marple mystery with a black-clothed priest hovering, goblet in hand, over a soon-to-be corpse.

She remembered that, as a child, she had done something wrong and Mother had used the word transgression. Julia had asked, 'What is transgression?'

'Go and look it up.'

So she had, lying on her tummy with her legs in the air with the falling-to-bits dark blue *Encyclopaedia Dictionary R–T.* She found the word between *transfusion* and *tranship* but then her eyes wandered and were fixed on *transhumance* next-but-one down: 'The seasonal migration of livestock and those who tend them between lowlands and adjacent mountains.'

She had ignored transgression.

Hadn't Dylan Thomas written a poem? Her memory was being too clever by half. 'I have longed to move away from the hissing of the spent lie… By these I would not care to die, Half convention and half lie.'

Perhaps she could have read English literature at university?

How she now longed for a belly-aching good laugh at something which wasn't rude, designed to humiliate, or so dirty that watching it on television in the company of others made everyone embarrassed. Although she never admitted it out loud, she could understand why those butchering Islamist caliphates saw the west as a threat. Surely there was a middle way.

She had almost given up on television and would have done so had it not been for that nice, good-looking Simon Reeve and Brian Cox, who made her feel young again.

'Hi, Gran. How are things? I thought you'd like to know you're going to be a great-grandmother in August. I am sending you a photo of the two-month scan as an email attachment.'

Her second grandson, who rarely phoned, sounded pleased so Julia tried to sound pleased too but this news immediately put her into a spin for she was still worrying about overpopulation and the difficulties of downloading anything from her computer. The prospect pushed her immediately into a mode of self-doubt and inadequacy and she asked herself the question: 'What have you ever done in your life?'

Well, there had been the odd charitable committee to which she had offered her services, small-scale local issues which interested her, but she probably got involved purely from a sense of her own guilt rather than because of the cause itself.

On the plus side, she had produced a family which had reproduced itself and her thoughts might be carried on by them, especially by Harry. Now they were all dispersed, integrated and absorbed into other people's families, immersed in hectic lives, contacting her only in an emergency and accepting modern digital technology as if it were the word of God.

She looked at the poster of Fra Angelico's Annunciation on the wall of her bedroom. It always gave her a feeling of calm, of acceptance. She had had the fresco enlarged from a postcard bought at the Museo del Convento di San Marco on that tiring, hot, touristy visit to Florence a quarter of a century ago, in a distant time when she thought she was still young but was really middle aged. She had stayed with Bill and Jane, old friends of Hugh's, in their beautiful home in Tuscany. Now, like Hugh, they were gone.

She had created her own fresco, what she called her 'love wall', in the kitchen. It was a mosaic of drawing pins, Blu-Tack, cobwebs and dust; photos of the children and grandchildren as babies, toddlers, teenagers, in mortar boards and gowns, getting married, a tapestry of smiling faces which gave Julia a sense of wellbeing and still belonging. She had chosen the happy times, avoiding reality and the grubby little secrets hidden beneath, the dark hurts and injustices and personal traumas.

She would make an effort to spend her remaining years

trying to be joyful. When she awoke not wanting to get out of bed, dreading what the lonely day had on offer, she would give herself a quick talking to. Just existing should be sufficient but mankind had demanded more. There were those to whom existence had, of necessity, been their all. Why, immediately, did her mind flit to Belsen…?

She felt hungry and couldn't be bothered to make a sandwich. Remembering that there were the remains of a roast chicken in the fridge, she tore it limb from limb, eating everything, exploring under each bone for a piece of flesh, leaving only the skeleton and dark red congealed innards on the plate. In Belsen those too would have been fought over.

She looked again at the photos on the wall. There was a recently added one of Matt and he always cheered her up. He was wearing alien clothes, a smart but ill-fitting suit bought in haste from M&S when he had been summoned to London to attend a small exhibition of his paintings. Like Julia, he did not enjoy dressing up to try and become something he was not but Harry and Anna had persuaded him to go. Anna said that it was one of those one-off opportunities thrown up by life, which needed to be grabbed at and garnered, which could have unexpected consequences further down the line. But Matt was already further down the line, was content and really had no need for further consequences.

CHAPTER 7

Few people knew that Matt was an artist; his talent was hidden beneath the rough exterior he showed to the world. He was well known for his livestock. He bred bulls which he sold privately; he abhorred the big pedigree sales where unrealistic prices into the tens of thousands gave the auctioneer a huge rake off and the vendor was obliged to give half of it back in 'luck money' to the buyer. Never quite getting the amount right caused resentment, a sort of 'I'll buy your bull if you buy mine' syndrome.

Amongst his regular buyers, Matt had a small group of clients who were not real farmers like himself but land agents, estate and farm managers who worked for other people. The exorbitant price of land and shortage of farms to tenant excluded them from getting on the bottom rung of the agricultural ladder, and they counted themselves lucky to have found jobs with millionaires from the City and celebrities who thought it would be cool and enhance their environmental image if they could show their love of wildlife and the countryside by owning a good slice of it. Many of their camp followers were into animal rights; balaclava-clad, they rampaged through the countryside at weekends, causing havoc, protesting in exchange for free transport and thirty quid.

Matt possessed that gut instinct of knowing the real value of things. Alongside his commercial beef herd of Charolaise, he bred some impressive Longhorn cattle and rare breeds of sheep – Jacobs, Soays, Whitefaced Woodlands. New breeds of landowners liked something old and different to show off on their land. Matt had also found a profitable side line supplying these animals to television and film producers to authenticate rural backdrops; his Longhorn bull had appeared behind Colin Firth in *Pride and Prejudice.*

Asked into the house for a cup of coffee after a successful transaction, one of the buyers, whose employer was lead guitarist with a well-known pop group and had a penchant for badgers, commented on the paintings on the walls. 'Those are good, really lifelike. My boss would love the badger ones. Who is the artist?'

'Well, I am, when I have the time.'

Matt found it difficult to keep off the subject of badgers. He saw the beauty of them as he did in all things feral but badgers were his neighbours from hell, plundering nests and devouring the eggs of skylarks, curlews and any ground-nesting birds they could get their jaws into.

In the old days his father had kept a Sealyham terrier, tough bred and hardy, to take on the jaws of a badger. These dogs were a rare breed now, incompatible like himself to the twittering of a sentimentalised, urban population. No longer permitted to do what they were born for, they had become poodles of the catwalk, strutting at Cruft's, all instinct knocked out of them. But when they were asleep, Matt thought, like himself they could still dream, on the scent of prey, their paws twitching with the excitement of the chase, giving little yelps of delight; a quick bite at the throat and then the joy, rolling in badger shit and returning home to the envy and approbation of the dog next door and the disapproval of their owner and the stink of shampoo.

Matt had no wish to lock horns again with the animal-rights brigade whose understanding of animal cruelty was selective. Let them believe what they wanted; nature and the planet would survive long after Homo sapiens had destroyed themselves. And intelligent people would no longer be subjected to *Springwatch*, Bill Oddie wearing pristine clean wellies, what Anna called an 'Agnis' – All the Gear and No Idea.

There had been an unpleasant, disturbing event one Bank Holiday. Matt, driving the Land Rover and trailer, was aware that the traffic was heavier and faster than usual but unaware that it was a national holiday. He never had holidays; all days were the same to him. He noticed that the roadkill was more plentiful than usual: three pheasants, two badger cubs, a stoat and numerous rabbits within five miles. The crows, traffic wise, were snatching their meals from beneath car wheels, their raptor senses aware of approaching danger. They sat on the dry stone walls to await their chance, as they did at lambing time to peck out a tasty morsel of an eye from a half-born lamb as it emerged from the body of its prostrate mother.

Matt was driving too slowly for the holiday traffic building up behind him. One of the wheels on the trailer was a bit dodgy and he didn't want to give the police yet another reason to stop him. He was aware of the frustration of the other drivers. As he rounded a corner he saw in the distance, on the brow of the hill, a group of animals in the road. Not sheep, he thought, too big.

There did not appear to be a human with them. He thought a rambler must have left a gate open but, as he came nearer, he saw it was a small group of red deer, a fawn at the rear, her coat still retaining its juvenile spotted markings.

The car behind was blowing its horn. He heard the anger of a foot on an accelerator as it sped past him. A BMW, a World Wildlife Fund sticker in the rear window.

The deer were almost across when the fawn hesitated. Matt saw its mother turn her head to reassure and encourage it.

The BMW slammed into it but did not stop.

Matt jammed on his brakes. The car following him almost ran into him and stopped. In an instant he was on his knees with the fawn; its mother turned, gently hummering to it. He saw the two crushed legs and shattered body, the fawn struggling frantically to get up in answer to the mother's call. Matt bent down, cradling its body in his left arm, the soft velvet head against his stubbled cheek. He looked into the large, brown, trusting eyes and felt such love for it. With his right hand he drew his penknife from his pocket and slit its throat.

The occupants of the tailgating car got out. The young girl looked Indian; she had the same trusting, understanding eyes as the fawn. She was wearing what Matt thought was a sari; brown faces, other than those burnt by the elements, were scarce in his neck of the woods. How beautiful she was, he thought, all bright colours and elegance by the side of the road, folds of emerald silk edged with a strip of glittering golden braid caressing her body and head. What on earth was she doing there, so foreign on that bleak cold northern morning?

She knelt down on the hard road beside him and said, 'That was a brave and kind thing to do.'

She held her hands in supplication to give a blessing, a gentle whisper in a foreign tongue. He noticed the exquisite henna-painted patterns on her arms. How he would love to paint her. As her wrists moved, the gold bangles on her arms sounded a muffled tolling of bells. She reminded Matt of the young Indian girl, played by Jean Simmons in a film he had seen as a child, *The Black Narcissus*, an oasis in his teenage years when all had been drudgery and his fault, and his Nan had taken him to a matinee.

The male driver of the car was now standing over them. He was dressed in a smart suit and tie. 'Let me help you carry the body away from danger, for the mother will return to grieve. We can put it over the fence.' He introduced himself. 'I am Dr Caleb and this is my daughter. I am taking her to the Mela in Newcastle. She is meeting with many friends; last year it was cancelled because of the mud.'

They shook hands. 'Matt O'Brien, I farm around here.'

A second car had stopped, its driver curious and complaining. The blonde passenger was smoking a cigarette; her tight-fitting leather mini skirt made her exit from the car an ugly spectacle.

'We saw what you did. Disgusting! Animal murderer! We've taken the number of your car and we're going to report you to the RSPCA.' She took her mobile from her bag. Matt noticed it was made of deerskin.

He turned back to speak to the Indian girl but she had returned to the car and was already fastening her seat belt. Two cultures joining with a click. She wound down the window. Her painted hand rested on the sill. He put his own hand over it and felt its humanity – then she was gone.

'Those pictures would be a wow in London. My boss would love the badger paintings. I could try and persuade him to have a small exhibition for you. He has lots of friends with galleries in Duke Street, and he has contacts at the Tate. He mixes in those circles.'

Matt had been unsure; he had never been further south than Builth Wells to the Royal Welsh Show with his Kerry sheep and felt disorientated in a city larger than Carlisle. But then a letter arrived from the lead guitarist, personally signed.

Harry said, 'Gosh, Dad, can I have that letter with his autograph to show my friends at school? It will give me street cred. Do go, Dad. It will be fun and you've always said you wanted to see the world. This would be a start – and the band might be there and you might even speak to them and get their autographs for me.'

Matt had felt obliged to please Harry.

The first Julia heard about it was a Facebook message from Harry. *Gran, Dad has been invited to London to show his paintings in a gallery. I really would love him to go, it would do him good to have a break. I can help Mum with the livestock but as you know, Dad is incapable of going on his own and would get lost. He doesn't even possess a watch, let alone a mobile. He will be completely out of his depth and wouldn't know how to get a taxi in London even it came up to him with its lights flashing. You know he still tells the time by the position of the sun.*

This was true, not taking the mickey but a hard fact, for Matt could tell the time, give or take ten minutes, by the position of the sun in the daytime and the moon and stars at night.

Don't suppose, Gran, that you could go with him and hold his hand? It might be quite fun.

For a moment Julia thought about holding Matt's hand and quickly said yes. Of course it should have been the other way around, but hadn't Churchill once said 'Old age is not for wimps'?

Julia, approaching ninety, was out of touch with London; she hadn't visited for years and, if she had allowed herself to be honest, felt no wish to do so. Her last foray there had been in 2002, when she had joined half a million country dwellers marching in defence of liberty, livelihood and a way of life they believed in. They had been ignored, though there had been one good outcome. In her twilight years, on that march, Julia had met the love of her life. But that was another story.

She knew she would find it difficult to feel at ease, to adapt to the sea of multi-cultural faces and different tongues which would now assail her. The memories of three-quarters of a century ago were stronger than those of yesterday. Notting Hill Gate, war-blitzed, shabby, the sleazy hostel land of her youth. Yes, Christie had murdered all those women just around the corner and poor simple Timothy Evans had been hung for it, but all that shabbiness was comfortably reassuring. There were no feelings of having to compete; there was a shared resilience. Your neighbours needed you just as much as you needed them and, other than the wide boys, spivs and arms dealers who had made money out of the war, Londoners were still in it together. Julia knew she would not like the smart, divided place the city had allowed itself to become, where oligarchs had made it their home, their gold dust settling like a choking ash over W1.

She and Matt made an early start from the Citadel station. They planned to be there and back in the day, neither wishing to make an outing out of it, both secretly wishing – but neither admitting it to the other – that they had not made the decision to go. They sat opposite one another, fortunate to have window seats. The carriage was almost empty; backpackers and ramblers waited at Oxenholme station to join before the influx at Preston.

She remembered different rail journeys, wretched and lonely, back to the bleak winter term of boarding school, discipline and lacrosse. Forced to leave behind freedom and the warmth and magic of the summer holidays. The clickety-click of wheels passing over points.

She remembered another age, when her small hands struggled, trying to lift upwards the thick, hardened leather straps of the carriage window to release it, leaning out as far as she dared to turn the heavy brass handle on the outside, panicked by its stiffness. Would anyone know she was there? Would the guard check? Or would the whistle blow and she be carried off to goodness knows where? The smell of steam and coal smoke, small cinders of ash in her eyes and the smell of dried urine rising from the track from the constant dripping of the WCs, like the latrines of some mediaeval moving castle. Now there would be confusing buttons to press, everything encased and under someone else's control.

The pendolino tilted and twisted like some great serpent, swaying its way through the countryside, making Julia feel sick and unable to read her book. Should she go to the loo now, before they reached Preston and the carriage became crowded? She could lose her balance and wasn't certain at which end of the compartment the lavatory was situated, so she looked out of the window instead.

Trees, fields, hamlets, hedgerows and homesteads blurred by at speed; there was no time to gaze upon and enjoy them, the whoosh of haste inviting heads to loll and minds to be lulled into their dream worlds.

Was she dreaming? Was she again on her way back to school, with that empty feeling in the pit of her stomach, carrying her suitcase with a luggage label tied to its handle saying who she was up the steep hill to the school gates with their impressive ornamental iron work, the school motto in foot high capitals wrought into the carvings of Welsh dragons: 'Deo Soli Sit Honor Et Gloria'.

In that hallucinatory moment of half sleep, as she tried to make herself come awake, the words had changed to 'Arbeit Macht Frei'.

Her eyes opened momentarily but long enough to imprint on her dozing mind the figure of a man standing between wind-bent willows on the bank of a small river, fishing rod in hand, casting against the wind. Surely it was her father? Even half dreaming, she knew it couldn't be.

In her drowsy state, she wondered what fly the fisherman was using. A snipe and purple, a partridge and red, or perhaps a Greenwell's glory. The names held a nostalgic magic. What fun she and her father had together, tying flies, the choice so important, judging the weather and the river's flow before decisions were made where to cast. Moments of joy which now hurt, for there were other moments best forgotten.

Because it was wartime, games fields across the land had been commandeered for food production, 'dug for victory' to plant vegetables and wheat. The school had negotiated a deal with the Ministry of Food to graze sheep rather than sacrificing the school pitches to the plough. The school was known for its sportiness and the headmistress, Beatrice Tomlinson MA (Oxon), had dug in her toes.

Before the whistle blew for the start of a lacrosse match, there was the sheep shit to clear from the pitch. Participants were given a bucket and a stick. Those with savvy went for the firm droppings, easily speared, but the majority were of an unpleasant consistency from sheep that were obviously unwell. Julia, brought up on a farm, was all too familiar with bits of tapeworm and the symptoms of Johne's disease, gastro-intestinal helminthiasis and nematodirus.

The girls conjured up clever ways to avoid sheep-shit duty. You could be excused from games if you had the curse. Matron, nicknamed Bella, checked carefully the mandatory curse date-book. You could get away with having the curse twice monthly for a certain period but, if it became a habit, you were hauled off to see an unpleasant gynaecologist in Chester.

Julia thought that when she got home she must tell Harry about 'school sheep-shit duty'. It would give him a good laugh. She knew exactly what his reaction would be:

'Health and safety would have a field day, Granny.'

The carriage was filling up. A surge of people got on at Preston, desperate mothers battling with pushchairs and luggage, the paraphernalia which Mothercare insisted they must have. But the pendolino had the bit between its teeth and was not going to let them settle down; it had targets, timetables and shareholders.

The influx awoke Matt and he left his seat to help. Standing in no man's land, that unstable area where the carriages joined, Matt thought he saw the Indian girl through the glass partition, a splash of colour and a dark skin. The automatic doors opened; it was not the Indian girl but a large smiling black lady with a child in her arms. So far as he could see, she had no luggage. Her headdress of bright orange and green matched the voluminous swathes of mammy cloth which engulfed her body.

Matt took the child from her arms and instinctively kissed the black forehead and smelled the sweetness of her skin. He noted her hair, beribboned and tightly plaited in a hundred strands. He said, 'I like your hair. What pretty ribbons.'

The child smiled back, her large brown eyes trusting with the unsullied honesty of the very young. He had seen that look before in newspapers. There had been that child who looked so similar, Victoria Climbié. His mind wept at the thought, at the same time wondering how long it had taken to weave the tiny plaits. Had the mother got up early? Perhaps it was permanent, allowed under a different culture to remain unwashed. He kissed the child's forehead again and placed her in the seat next to him as the large lady shuffled and squeezed her voluptuous body into the seat next to Julia.

On the other side of the coach, two small girls with painted fingernails and dummies in their mouths were being shouted at by their mother as she struggled to find a space to leave the pushchair. It was obvious to Julia that they could not hear her for their ears were wired up to something and Julia could hear the pulsating throb of Madonna singing 'I Am a Material Girl'.

As the train started to move, the mother rolled her eyes in Matt's direction with a disapproving look and turned her attention to the elderly man asleep in one of her reserved seats. He was probably dreaming dreams, as Julia was.

'Excuse me.' Her voice aggressive. But he was somewhere else. 'EXCUSE ME, are you deaf or something?'

Matt stood up to offer assistance but sat down again. He was hemmed in by the child and if he got up now it would just cause more confusion. Almost before she sat down, the African lady had reached under her voluminous garments and produced a thin colouring book and a cheap packet of five wax crayons. The child studied the picture intently and reached for the yellow crayon. Matt remembered wax crayons from his own childhood; they broke easily and it was difficult to produce good definition because the colour slithered away across the page and not where you wanted to put it.

Even upside down he could see that it was a picture of Christ, Holman Hunt's painting of *The Light of the World*. The child had almost finished the halo and the lantern. He noticed the palms of her hands were pink and wondered why.

He asked, 'Do you believe in God?'

She looked up, smiled and said, 'Yes.' She smiled again, looked up at the African lady who nodded. 'Pentecostal.'

The mother with the two children across the way heard the question and turned away, rolling her eyes again. The old man had apologised and relinquished his window seat.

At a diagonal on the other side of the carriage, a man was reading a newspaper. Now fully awake, Julia read the two-inch headline: 'Prestigious Girls School Bites the Dust'. Julia took her long-distance glasses out of her bag to read the sub-headlines 'Scandal and fraud: parents given one week's notice'. Why Julia imagined it might be her old school she did not know but she was certain it was; the daydreaming held significance. If the man abandoned his newspaper, she would ask Matt to reach over and ask to borrow it.

From the age of ten, the school motto and the philanthropy of the school's benefactor had been drilled into Julia once a week for six years at school assembly; the Welshman had almost become part of Julia's extended family. A sixteenth-century merchant adventurer from the City of London, the benefactor had made his fortune trading with Spain and Portugal. Being childless, he had bestowed 12,000 golden ducats (£2.2 million in today's money), the proceeds of this fortune to be given each year to educate four maiden orphans of his lineage. If these could not be found, four maiden orphans of any lineage sufficed until, after three hundred years, no maiden orphans at all could be found. In 1858 an Act of Parliament was passed, empowering the Court of Chancery to extend the trust to establish a girls' school. At ten years old, this fairy tale of chivalry had charmed Julia but years of repetition had made it lose its appeal. She still retained an imagery of this sixteenth-century philanthropist in her mind; a benevolent face. He bore a striking resemblance to Matt.

Sitting directly opposite him, it was the first time Julia had had an opportunity to study Matt's face. They met frequently but it was always in the rush of survival and obligation, his face animated and on the move. Now it was at rest, in repose, and she had the chance to sit and stare. At sixty-eight years old, he hadn't a grey hair in that mop of long conker-coloured curls, no sign of balding or receding. Like an ageing pop star, his face was grooved and ravaged, not by drugs but by the elements; it was weather-battered, like a much-travelled old leather suitcase still carrying the torn off, scuffed labels of a hard life, difficult to read, addresses worn and smudged. His eyes had a depth and calmness to them which made you feel that he was elsewhere, thinking different thoughts, unaware of his surroundings. He was nearer to her age than he was to Anna's and that was perhaps why Julia felt such an affinity with him – and she also had witnessed his nudity. He had the type of face costume drama producers looked for when casting a Thomas Hardy novel She wondered whether he was aware of how physically attractive he was to her.

The train was filling up, a surge of people battling to get on. Now the faces were not white and Julia wondered why on earth they wanted to exchange blue skies and sun for the underground Hades of Birmingham New Street. Was the grass always greener?

The man with the newspaper had alighted, leaving it on his seat. Matt stretched over, grabbed it and handed it to Julia.

Pages two and three gave all the details. The school was now on the market for £2.2 million and appeared to be owned by someone with an address in the Cayman Islands. Julia read further; there had been inappropriate behaviour from both pupils and staff, though the paper didn't go into detail. Court cases were still pending. Probably crushes which had got out of hand, as they had in her day. But the main reason for the school's closure was a totally new phenomenon: a list of wrongful dismissal claims had been taken to court and won, leaving the school bankrupt.

Julia was reminded of the court case facing Matt on their return north. She worried about how Harry would stand up under cross-examination. She put the whole episode to the back of her mind to be brought forward later.

With his eyes, Matt asked the child whether he might borrow the red and blue wax crayons. She understood and smiled. He took an old envelope from his pocket and within five minutes produced a portrait of her.

From the relative relaxation of the train to be plunged suddenly into Euston station with its overcrowded bustle, where everyone appeared to be sure of their destination, made Julia's glaucoma play up. She could not focus on anything.

She saw the reassuring red, yellow and blue sign of Burger King with relief; at least they could pop in and have something to eat. Burger land was familiar to Matt; he would feel at home there rather than in the sophistication of upmarket bistros and Julia had always enjoyed unpretentious eating.

Getting a taxi was easier than she had anticipated. There was a large sign saying taxi rank and an orderly queue.

When she was young she had been adept at whistling one up, something Father had taught her: two fingers in the mouth and tongue pressed hard against the roof of the mouth, the same technique he used to whistle up rats. Standing in the hay barn with a 2.2 rifle, picking them off as they emerged to investigate the high-pitched sound.

They arrived at the gallery at just about the right time. There was already the hum of conversation from inside. Julia quickly manoeuvred Matt past the liveried doorman for she knew his habit of stopping to pass the time of day lengthily with everyone. They were greeted by a smiling waitress carrying a tray of champagne in tall thin flutes from which, if you had a large nose, it was impossible to drink. Matt was already making the waitress laugh with his remarks, the glass invisible within his huge hand, sure of himself as he always was.

Julia was trying to get him into the adjoining room where she could see vaguely familiar minor celebrity faces clad in Armani and tarty Versace. There were one or two all-too-familiar old ones from the BAFTA awards in 2004, when the Countryside Alliance had won and they had shown their displeasure by booing. Matt and she were in alien territory.

Everyone seemed to know everyone else, calling each other 'darling' in that false way Julia remembered when Hugh had come close to becoming a tycoon in the life she had abandoned half a century ago.

Matt's paintings were exhibited in a small anteroom off the main gallery. One or two women wandered through; they all looked like Kate Middleton and said, 'Oh how cute,' when they looked at the picture of a fox. Two badger painting had red sold stickers on them; the one of the rat, which Julia thought was by far the best because Matt had captured perfectly the astute intelligent look in its eyes, was not attracting attention.

Julia returned to the foyer to find Matt. He and the waitress were in animated conversation. Matt said, 'Come and meet Leanne. She comes from Bishop Auckland and her grandfather still lives in Low Etherly. My father once bought a really good Swaledale tup from him. She's only doing this job to get herself through university.'

Julia suddenly had the urge to kiss Leanne, which she did, for she knew Leanne had made Matt's journey south worthwhile.

She took Matt's arm and said, 'Come on, we need to circulate,' the memories of her duty as a company wife coming to the fore.

They entered the main gallery and Matt instantly recognised a woman with wild hair whom he had seen on a newsreel some years ago, standing beside a slummy, unmade double bed. People were talking in an animated, excited way and he and Julia edged in to take a closer look. Gary Finkelstein, the gallery owner, a short man with a sallow complexion, greased-back long hair and protruding eyes, was effervescing about a heap of sawdust with dark lumps in it that looked like sheep shit.

Matt murmured, 'The emperor's new clothes.'

Julia looked in her catalogue. 'Number 131, "Nature's Bounty". Price estimate £500,000.'

They caught the late Virgin Express train from Euston and arrived in Carlisle around midnight, both having decided that it would be their last visit to London.

On the news three days later it said that a work of art sold in London for three-quarters of a million pounds and there was a picture of the sawdust.

Matt went outside to the shed to bed down the cattle. He shovelled the sawdust out of the trailer. Normally the cattle were bedded on straw but the exceptionally wet summer had made the price of straw exorbitant, and the small cottage industry making wooden rakes in the neighbouring village was pleased to get rid of surplus wood shavings. They had a flourishing export business, sending their handmade wooden hay rakes to Eastern European countries in exchange for their people, who were more than happy to get their hands dirty.

CHAPTER 8

Julia tried to be fair about how many photos there were of everyone on the wall. Complaints had been made that some family members were under-represented and she had searched in drawers to find suitable ones to salve their egos. She had found a lovely one of her daughter-in-law, John's wife, smiling and showing the confidence she exuded. People popping in for a coffee at Julia's kitchen table asked, 'Who is that lovely girl? Is that one of your daughters?' Julia could not understand why her daughter-in-law so disliked the photo.

You had to be so careful with daughters-in-law, take a course in diplomacy before the first visit. Learn to bite your tongue and hope that their standard of domesticity was as negligent as your own, that they'd share the joke when offered a cup of coffee in a mug which said 'Only dull women have tidy houses', and agree with your belief that a bit of dirt around the place would do miracles for the maturing of your grandchildren's immune systems. It had been a bit of a let-down that these qualities were absent in her daughter-in-law.

It came to light when, after that first awkward visit, Julia could not find the tea towels which had been there at lunchtime; admittedly they had a few holes in them, hadn't been washed for some time and resembled grey rags. Julia later found them in the dustbin, together with a heavy-duty potato masher, its rusty patches hardly noticeable, a family heirloom of which she was particularly fond. It held happy memories – she remembered Nellie the cook using it in the forties, producing magic wormed potatoes. Julia fished it out of the dustbin and gave it a rinse under the hot tap but left the tea towels where they were and decided to try harder in the cleanliness department.

Looking at the photos on the wall, she thought what a curious assortment of minds her now dried-up womb had produced all those years ago. If she were honest, there were more pictures of Harry than her other grandchildren. Sometimes she felt she was seeing Harry through rose-tinted specs; other family members hinted at it. Were all his loving Facebook messages thought up and sent to Granny to keep her on his side?

A sense of urgency, a quick realisation that her time was almost up, overwhelmed her. There were millions of her contemporaries out there, struggling with the same dilemmas, approaching the end of their lives and asking themselves what it had all been about. Before she could answer that question, she must try and get rid of the detritus from the past which still clogged her own life.

It was Harry who, two years after Hugh's death, encouraged her to 'move forward' in the media speak he had picked up from politicians and others anxious to forget the past. But the past was now all that Julia had.

Harry was in his early teens when Hugh died and on the cusp of manhood. He regretted that he had spent so little time with his grandfather. His paternal grandparents had died before Harry was even conceived. At school he had once written an essay, three hundred words about childhood. He had written an outpouring of grief for someone he loved but never got to know. He got an A star.

'I loved it, Granny, when Grandpa said, "Come into my study, I've got something to show you." It's an Aladdin's cave of interesting things in there.'

Hugh had taught Harry how to tie knots, a skill Hugh had learned at Dartmouth Naval College in the thirties when he was a midshipman. The knots had appealing names which fired and excited the imagination: a Rogue's Knot, a Surgeon's Knot, a Tom Fool's Knot, even a Granny Knot. There were hitches too: a Slippery Hitch, a Clove Hitch, a Lark's Head Hitch and a False Lark's Head Hitch. Of course these things could now be learned on the internet but what Harry loved was the feel of Grandpa's gnarled old fingers and his own, entwined to get the knot right.

Julia had not wanted to explore Hugh's study too quickly out of a kind of respect for someone she had found difficult to live with. The room was piled high with his life into which she had been denied entry, the untidiness and hoarding of his final years hiding the well-organised files beneath, dementia creeping up on him like 'grandmothers' footsteps'. He had left her without a word, slumped over the kitchen table, bogged down by bureaucratic paperwork over which he had once been so meticulous, surrounded by incomprehensible pencil-scribbled notes on backs of envelopes.

Harry was with her when she finally felt strong enough to venture inside Hugh's domain. The solid brass handle of the study door was stiff, its interior workings rusty through lack of use.

Harry said, 'Let me have a go, Gran.'

He had his father's strong hands. Together they pushed the door; it opened five or six inches then stopped. Something was wedged against it.

Julia instantly thought it was Hugh's body. After all, she hadn't buried him on the high fells above their house, the place of his choice. She heard his voice again: 'Keep out.'

Harry squeezed his hand around the door. 'It feels like a heap of old newspapers.' He pulled at something, tearing the cover off *The Sunday Times* magazine dated May 2 1976, with a photograph of Lord Montgomery on the front. Harry asked, 'Who was Lord Montgomery?'

Julia said, 'Well, let's fish out the other pages and have a look.'

Harry had wanted to know all about General Montgomery, which held them up for some time. Julia recognised now how justified Hugh had been in his hoarding for he had understood that sparks of understanding must be ignited by something.

In their sixty-four years of togetherness, Hugh had never thrown anything away. He, like Julia, had been brought up to be thrifty; now obsolescence was built into everything in order to make people spend, spend, spend. It was a policy which was supposed to make Britain great again but as far as Julia could see, all it did was drag the country further into the quicksand of globalisation and debt. The environmentalists would have you believe that all this was destroying the planet but Julia had seen nature at close hand, having lived in its palm all her life; she knew it would bounce back, evolve and survive long after the human race had destroyed itself.

It was not only newspaper cuttings that Hugh had kept but boxes and boxes of undated and unclassified photos of strangers and places, videos and travel brochures from the 1950s. Hugh's library was extensive; he kept newspapers mainly for their obituaries, the successes, notoriety and aspirations of contemporaries, lives he had briefly brushed against. When time allowed, he had cut them out to put in books where the person was mentioned; he said it would add to their value when he got down to cataloguing the books – which he never did. Julia had the guilty feeling that she should do the cataloguing; after all, these paper records had been Hugh's overwhelming passion and she must remain true to his wishes.

He also kept pieces of copper piping, portions of plastic hose, bed springs, old gate hinges still attached to gates, old batteries ranging in size from tractor to mobile phone, cigarette cards and jigsaws from his childhood. All these things were adding to the turmoil in Julia's mind; not only was she having to deal with the detritus, the flotsam and jetsam of a lifetime with Hugh that she was trying to make sense of, she was also trying to stem the incoming tide of Anna, Matt and Harry's problems.

When finally the door was fully open, the heat from the room was stifling. Julia had forgotten that there was a low-powered heater left on permanently to protect Hugh's books, to keep them at a comfortable temperature. It was a comfort Julia had been denied in her bedroom; no wonder the electricity bills about which Hugh complained had been astronomic.

A thick layer of dust covered everything. It would take a day or two to make a pathway through the piles of papers and books to the window where the curtains, which had never been drawn, had perished decades ago and were hanging in shreds. Once upon a time they were bright orange, trendy, a relic of the sixties. They had been altered and moved thriftily from house to house, their dimensions changed by the old Singer sewing machine which had lived most of its life in India and bore the ravages of travel. Hugh's mother had owned it when she was a dutiful memsahib in colonial days.

The inside of the study windows were moss-grimed, covered in dead flies, spiders and woodworm beetles. They reminded Julia of Miss Havershams's cobwebbed wedding cake in that black-and-white David Lean film of the 1940s. Valerie Hobson played Estella; like Julia, Valerie Hobson had stuck by her man.

Julia touched her wedding ring, loose now on a skeletal finger, held in place by arthritic swollen joints. She turned it full circle and thought how miraculous it was that she and Hugh had reached their diamond wedding anniversary.

Still hanging on its solid brass hook behind the door was his old Barbour, worn and cuffs frayed. Pinned to the left lapel were the icons of his life: the Arctic Star, the DSO, the British Legion, No to Maastricht, Not in My Name. She buried her head deep in the jacket and smelt Hugh again, his scent still strong like an old dog fox. In her imagination she touched him intimately, her caressing hand knowing how he liked it. She remembered that hope of the bliss of togetherness which their minds could never find.

For the first time in years she wept uncontrollably, remembering how the doctor, police and undertakers had all come too quickly before she had found the right moment to explain to Hugh that she understood the demon he had within him which swallowed up his feelings for his family, that parasitic worm which turned him into the kind of person he had no wish to be. Now, clearing his study, Julia read copies of personal letters written to his friends. He had found himself too late and she wept for the sadness of how he must have felt with that knowledge.

Harry put his arm around her and said, 'I know Gran.'

But how could he know?

Over the following days, she made a start, putting aside fifty-year-old bank statements for Harry to feed into the shredder during the holidays, making irreversible decisions about what to keep or not. And she developed a respect for Hugh which she had not allowed herself when he was alive.

He had kept all those letters from little people. Amongst the correspondence from politicians and the famous, it was the humanity, the humility in those ill-educated pencilled words, written with such care on lined paper, which surprised Julia. He had put them in a special file with the word 'KEEP' in large black capitals. Other people had loved him dearly, seen a different person; their distance made them see him more clearly, they had been part of an emotional life denied to his family.

She remembered her mother, whom Hugh had described as a difficult woman, saying, 'Poor Hugh, he cannot accept the joy of living.'

Underneath more recent hoardings, made when his

mind was going and he dumped things anywhere, she came across a receipt from the Savoy Hotel dated 1950. It was for the first night of their honeymoon, when they could still laugh together. She recalled that the wardrobe was almost as large as their first rented home and that there had been problems with the plumbing; oil was coming up the plug hole of the bath. There was something about a still-active Nazi bomb being found on the Embankment and the bomb-disposal team and a plumber were sent for. Instead of getting into bed to surrender her maidenhead, she and Hugh had had to wait for a plumber. She believed that plumbers were still in short supply in London.

She knew that she would now have to read everything in case she threw herself away. In doing so, perhaps for the first time she would meet the man to whom she had been married for so long, or at least that part of him which he had found impossible to share with her. He had lived an emotionally aloof life, surrounded by his possessions, his family witnessing his unhappiness. His study was where his mind had lived separately from theirs and on his death she felt a duty to try and understand it.

Memory is so selective, conspiratorial, with thoughts coming from different directions, judgemental at the moment of implant until time and wisdom give it a chance to reassess itself, just as Julia was now doing through necessity.

She had put out six blue bags of what she hoped the council would accept as domestic rubbish, feeling she was letting Hugh down. He had never forgiven her for throwing away his old digger hat, a present from an Aussie Japanese POW who was being repatriated to Sydney at the end of the war in the Pacific in 1945. Julia had tried to defend her action but he rejected her explanation that it was full of moth grubs.

She heard the recycling carts approach and ran outside, shouting, trying to stop them but it was too late. They were gone in an instant and hadn't heard her calls; her voice had been deadened by the sound of the truck's engine and the grinding machinery grabbing all those memories as though they didn't matter. Her life with Hugh was about to be recycled into heaven knew what.

And it had been on that day, as she returned to the house, she heard the phone ringing. Anna's hysterical voice, 'Matt's been beaten up, he's got a broken jaw. He's in hospital. I've rung the police.'

This time there had been a witness. Harry, cycling home from school, was humming Glenn Miller's 'Moonlight Serenade'. He enjoyed the softness of muted brass, it was comforting. He also liked Elvis and was saving up his pocket money for a pair of blue suede shoes.

Turning up the lane, he saw three men in the distance. As he came closer, trying to avoid the potholes, he saw that one was his father lying on the ground, his arms outstretched, trying to ward off the blows from the other two.

He shouted at the top of his voice, 'Stop it, stop it! Leave him alone!' The men turned; it was his uncle Theo and cousin Piers, who already had a reputation for beating up girlfriends and was known to social services.

'Fuck off, you little bastard! It will be your turn next,' Piers yelled.

Harry threw his bike down and raced towards them.

Although he was only fifteen he was already six feet tall and, on seeing him approach, the two men stopped the assault. Harry rushed at them and landed a left hook on Piers, who fell back. It was the first time Harry had been allowed to test his physical strength against another human being and it felt good, for it was in a just cause.

Blood was streaming from his father's face and his eyes were already swelling from the pummelling onslaught. His jaw looked lopsided but it was the damage to his father's hands which distressed Harry, those reliable strong, good hands that had tried to defend their owner and had taken the brunt of the attack.

He used his mobile first for an ambulance, then the police. They arrived within fifteen minutes but the attackers were long gone.

After seeing his father safely into the ambulance, Harry returned to the house to tell Anna what had happened. He was followed by the police car. This time the police were helpful. They took statements and asked, 'Do you want to press charges?'

Revenge was not a concept understood by Matt or Anna. Harry said, 'I think my uncle and cousin, and particularly Auntie Carla, need help.'

It was decided to take no further action but in Carla's eyes turning the other cheek was a sign of weakness and she was practised at exploiting weakness. It was a lesson she had learnt in childhood and altering the truth had become second nature.

The summons arrived on the doorstep of Green Syke the same morning as a heavy package was left in Julia's post box, the old metal ammunition box rescued from a battleship which Hugh had painted black and utilised.

The package contained brochures. Julia had perhaps been premature in contacting McCartney Stone who offered luxury, independent living for the elderly. Their persuasive television advertisements had tempted her and she had done it with the best of intentions, to do something about her future without burdening her young. The glossy brochure was impressive, offering her a secure, comfortable future. The company was building a development on the site of the old gas works which she remembered from her youth. Then she had been fascinated by how the centre of the circular steel structures containing the gas went up and down, rising like giant cupcakes.

She stroked the seductive glossy brochure and touched the architect's drawing of the trees. They were not the trees she knew that whispered and shouted with the wind, talking to her every day.

When the phone went, she jumped. Once again Anna's voice had that hysteria below the surface, a tight, just-about-under-control sound. 'You're not going to believe this, Mum, but Matt is being sued for assault and GBH by Theo and Piers.'

Chapter 9

Julia was beginning to have problems with old age. She was not just old but *really* old and it wearied her physically and unsettled her mind. She was disturbed by being taken back to the past, and the clarity of those reawakened memories. She had the opposite to dementia. Was there a special name for it? Had it been classified, given a nomenclature, to balance the opposite to being senile or insane? She had no wish to give her condition a label but, should society and the media demand one in order that she could be identified like some geological rock strata, she was happy to go along with it. She had fun finding a suitable name which would fit the bill: 'octogenarian bipolar confabulation' slipped easily off the tongue. It would soon become OBC and could be added to the list of initials thrown out daily which nobody knew the meaning of.

Whoops, her thoughts had ended with a preposition. Mother would not have liked that. Only that morning, trying to do a bit of decluttering among her books, she had come across pencilled notes on scraps of paper in her mother's strong hand. They were tucked inside dusty books, unopened for half a century, which had found a home with Julia when Mother died. They were devalued in the eyes of antiquarian booksellers by the inscriptions written on flyleaves by friends and family long since gone that gave them their true value. 'Kathleen, from her Godfather, Christmas 1909'. Little instructive chiding rhymes, tucked into once-upon-a-time nursery favourites, *The Moon and Sixpence* and *Amelianne and the Green Umbrella*.

Julia held the fragile yellowed piece of paper in her hand and read its fading message.

In Cumberland we have a way of saying more than we should say
We tack a preposition on to sentences both short and long
For instance when Julia has lost her hat, she shouts, 'Oh bother, where's it at?'
And David answers, sad but true, 'Well, Julia where've you put it to?'
Such lazy speech I much deplore.
Don't let me hear it any more.

Mother had been a hard disciplinarian and the tree of life about which they had been taught was still bearing fruit although Mother, unlike Father, was incapable of lifting her eyes 'unto the hills'.

Sleeping at nights had become a problem, for Julia could not prevent herself dozing off during the daytime. Night dreams now were always nightmares from which she awoke sweating and exhausted, confused, unable to differentiate between the semi-conscious world she was trying to shake off and the physical grind of the day to which she would awake. And then there was the court case coming up and she worried that Harry, as the only witness, would crumple under some clever barrister's onslaught.

Tired, she had gone to bed after the six o'clock news and awoken three hours later, jolted by an horrendous, ridiculous dream. She had dreamt that she was part of troupe of comical entertainers, on stage in fancy costume to entertain and make people laugh. But as act followed act, no one was laughing. She glanced at her alarm clock, eight thirty, and thought what a good night's sleep she had had until that stupid dream had roused her. She looked at the sky, the curtains still open, the westerly pink evening glow telling her that her mind and body were out of kilter

Harry, under cross-examination, might use words or phrases which in her day had been quite acceptable, tripped off the tongue as clichés without any intention to offend or have connotations put upon them by overzealous busy bodies. 'Fly in the ointment': the animal rights lot wouldn't like that. 'Needle in a haystack'? 'Nigger in the woodpile'?

Harry had that feral gene of instinct and good sense, a mongrel stamina inherited from his father which would get him into trouble.

When Hugh was alive there had been a different purpose for her existence; his ailments and daily requirements kept her mind busy and she had little time to think about herself or others. She had kept her concerns about Harry to herself, not wanting to worry Hugh who, approaching ninety, had to be reminded who Harry was.

Chapter 10

The court case took place a few weeks before Christmas. Julia suspected that Carla was wishing that she had not pressed charges; now it was Anna who wanted it to go ahead. It might put an end to the harassment and verbal abuse which had become a daily occurrence. Anyway, it was now in the hands of the CPS and out of their control and there was no going back.

As the only witness to what had happened, Harry took the stand. The vagaries and elusive justice of contemporary British law had not been apparent to him. Brought up to believe that twelve good men and true still held sway, he opted to stand in the witness box and swear on the Bible, rejecting the anonymity on offer to him as a juvenile to give evidence from behind a screen and unaware that the Bible had long since lost its sanctity. Harry's father had the strength to look people in the eye, call a spade a spade, not beat about the bush because some solicitor anxious to make a financial killing was coaxing him to do otherwise. The truth could not be bought nor misinterpreted; true men like his dad would sort things out.

But Harry had not understood that the truth could be usurped, taken out of the minds of people who were easily swayed by a manipulative and malicious press. A barbaric social media waited in the wings, vultures ready to pick over the bones of his words, whipping decent people into a vortex of suspicion and down the black hole of accusation.

On day three of the trial, Harry entered the witness box with confidence. He knew that he would speak the truth, the whole truth and nothing but the truth. He understood the difference between right and wrong but not the duplicity of the law.

He smiled at the prosecuting lady barrister when she asked him to repeat his name. She was pretty with lovely hair; the presiding judge had asked her to remove her wig so as not to appear intimidating. A wig would not have worried Harry, in fact it would have been exciting, something to tell his friends about at school just like *Law and Order* on television. Then he noticed her eyes. There was no warmth or understanding in them and for the first time he felt uneasy. They were like Aunt Carla's eyes.

'You love your father, Harry, don't you?'

'Of course.'

'You would do anything for him?'

'Yes.'

'Would you tell lies to protect him?'

There was just the slightest hesitation before he answered no but it was enough to catch the attention of two jurors who would normally be watching *Judge Judy* or *Judge Rinder* at that time of day.

The barrister snapped back, 'You aren't sure, are you, Harry? I suggest to you that is just what you are doing.'

'No.'

In that instant, Harry knew he had lost control, realised too late that adults were not to be trusted and respected.

'That will be all.'

'But I saw them,' Harry protested.

The judge said, 'Thank you, Harry, you may stand down.'
And in that instant Harry changed.

His Facebook messages to Julia became angry, not
particularly with her for he still ended them *lots and lots of
love as always, Granny* but now the rows of yellow faces had
mouths which turned down.

The thought that he had let his father down obsessed
him; although the case had been thrown out, it did nothing
to prevent the press having a field day. 'Teenager Lies to
Protect Local Gypsy Father' intimated one headline.

Julia knew she had lost him but prayed it would only be
a temporary loss, that she would eventually say the right
thing which might haul him in again before he got too far
out to sea and was pulled down by an undercurrent of anger
and thoughts of revenge. The situation was compounded by
another article running concurrently in the same edition
of the newspaper. There was a photo under the headline
'Pillar of the Community Receives Award': Carla dressed
to the nines, shaking hands with the Lord Lieutenant.

'Dad, they wouldn't listen to me. Dad, Dad, they
wouldn't listen.'

Matt replied, 'So it has always been, son,' and stroked
Harry's mop of hair.

Julia's compass had been altered and she couldn't readjust
it; it no longer sent its quivering pointer to the North Pole.
Hugh had somehow changed its magnetic pull to make her
wary of people, to mistrust instead of trust, and it was quite

a challenge to pull against its influence.

She looked through the morning post, hoping to find a handwritten letter among the avalanche of commercial trash – something physical. And there it was, written in an elaborate copperplate hand that she did not recognise. She opened it with the anticipation of a child about to explore the contents of a Christmas stocking. Inside there was a note in the same calligraphic perfection and a photo. A small coloured smiling child with tightly plaited hair and pink ribbons who looked like Victoria Climbié.

Julia read the note. *I have just travelled again between Preston and Birmingham and it put it in my mind of our 'brief encounter'. Your company and that of your husband made the journey pleasant. Although we didn't talk, your husband made an impression on Zipponah and she wanted to send you this photo. I am en route to stay with my other family in Kenya, Zipponah and I fly out tomorrow. With kindest regards.*

It was an informal note but on the adjoining page was a stamp of officialdom: Kenyan representative of the Youth Commonwealth Gender Forum, Malta 2015 under the auspices of the Royal Commonwealth Society. Julia wondered how the woman had acquired her address. Had Julia, half awake, handed over one of those personalised stickers with robins on which the Red Cross kindly sent her every Christmas?

CHAPTER 11

Christmas was approaching again. It was a time Julia had once loved and looked forward to, but now she dreaded it because decisions had to be made. She had already decided to play her trump old age card, not to send cards to anyone unless they sent her one first which appeared to be accepted if you were over a certain age. The three children would all ask her to spend the festive season with them and she never doubted for one moment that they wanted her. She must make a choice and try not to offend any of them.

Now her wanderings were nocturnal and her dysfunctional body was in charge, reaching hourly for plastic potty under the bed. This had a lot to do with how she would decide to spend Christmas. Last year the stairs in Sarah's expensive Cambridge home had felt steeper; she had been forced to ascend them on her hands and knees, trying to go up when no one was around for fear of causing them concern. Those Christmases at Sarah's had been wonderful, with tickets for the Carols at King's available annually. But now the anxiety of travel negated the enjoyment and the thought of having to change trains at Birmingham New Street made her feel physically sick.

There was still the possibility of going to her son John and daughter-in-law, or to Anna. A choice between a clinically perfect show, spiritually sterile, garlands of artificial, heavily berried holly, mistletoe and yew everywhere. Christmas cards trailing the walls on red ribbons, the posh ones in prominent positions wanting to be seen. Not a needle on the floor from the fold-away Christmas tree, the tender succulent turkey swimming in a Nigella Lawson gravy surrounded by all the trimmings which hadn't been around in Julia's day. Perhaps she would plump for chaos with Matt, Anna and Harry. They were all so busy that when you arrived mid-morning on Christmas Day they had all but forgotten it was Christmas and were nowhere to be seen. On previous occasions that she had stayed with them, Julia had fished her wellies out of the boot of the car and gone searching for them; on more than one occasion she had found them in a shed with their arm up a cow's backside dealing with some obstetrical problem. She was greeted not by 'Happy Christmas, Mum,' but 'Thank goodness you're here. Would you dash into the house and rescue the turkey? It's in the top oven of the Aga and is probably a burnt offering by now.'

But when they had eventually sat down to dried-up turkey, Matt said, 'For what we are about to receive may the Lord make us truly thankful,' and meant it.

She decided that this year she would please herself. She would spend Christmas in the comfort of her own home, alone, and face the disapproval of the young. But at the last minute, she phoned the local hostelry and asked if they could fit her in for their special Christmas dinner at lunch time. Her luck was in; there had been a cancellation.

She sat in the corner of the festive room, pleased with her decision. The two pretty waitresses smiled with their eyes and Julia established that one came from Kracow in Poland and the other from somewhere in Lithuania, countries Julia wished she had found the time to visit. The Polish girl had beautiful high cheekbones, a structure so attractive in both their women- and menfolk. She remembered Vitold who was over in Britain during the War with the Free Polish Airforce. He had kissed her when she was fifteen with what she now knew to be a French kiss.

The large family party at the next door table laughingly raised their glasses. An elderly man at its head caught her eye and lifted his glass to her. She lifted hers back and smiled, turning up her hearing aid to become part of the laughter.

She picked up the shiny red cracker. The family party were already wearing their paper hats and taking photos on their mobiles. She tried to pull the cracker herself, fishing with her fingers into its interior from both ends to find the paper strip with the little firework device in the middle. She remembered how her brothers had secretly hoarded the leftover explosive bits from amongst the crumbs of half-eaten bread and the sharp broken shells of brazil nuts and walnuts seen only at Christmas. They had saved them up to make a mini explosion, setting fire to them in a jam jar in the yard and shouting to her, 'Stand clear!'

Her wrists were not strong enough to pull the paper ends. She caught the eye of the old man again; he was watching her struggling. He got up and came over and together they pulled the cracker. Out dropped two dice; a double six landed uppermost and they both laughed.

He said, 'Won't you join us?'

She thanked him and declined.

The paper hat was blue, it would suit her grey hair. It was a bit on the large side. She put it on at a rakish angle, one side touching an eyebrow, and felt quite jaunty and again listened to and enjoyed the laughter from the next table but no longer felt the need to be part of it. She no longer desired its intimacy. The old man lifted his glass to her again and she thought he mouthed, 'Like the hat,' but she wasn't certain.

She had enjoyed that Christmas.

CHAPTER 12

Julia would rather not have had Harry's future resting in her hands. She was having niggling doubts about the wisdom of having joined Facebook, an impulse which at the time had made her feel good. It made her believe she could hack technology and be a trendy grandmother and move with the times, but it had brought additional responsibilities and put her in the firing line. Now, not only was she having to deal with Harry's sense of injustice coming at her on line but also Anna's fury at her son having been wronged.

Before the court case Harry's messages had been fun and she had clicked on them with joy and pleasant anticipation. He had begun to take an interest in politics.

Hi, Granny. Did you watch that election debate on telly last night? The one without Cameron and Clegg and those three awful women hugging each other like a coven of witches. They reminded me of the witches in Macbeth. Ha ha ha.

Julia was greatly encouraged by this message. Harry appeared to be further advanced in political awareness than she had imagined and to be taking an interest in Shakespeare in whatever form was a great improvement over his last message on the subject.

When, a few weeks earlier, she had tentatively enquired about the set books for his GCSE English Literature, he replied, *Of Mice and Men which is interesting. And Macbeth which is a load of crap and written in language I don't understand.*

Should she warn him about sexism? You had to be so careful; there were penalties now for being honest and saying what you truly felt. But before Julia had a chance to reply to this latest encouraging message, others were building up in Harry's message box.

First witch, Granny: 'When shall we three meet again?'

Second witch, Granny: 'When the hurly-burly's done, when the battle has been won.'

Granny, the Third Witch doesn't get much of a look in. Probably Plaid Cymru. I have renamed Macbeth Millibeth or Macband. What do you think? I felt really sorry for Farage, they ostracised him because he calls a spade a spade. Do you think he is a Banquo or a Duncan, Granny?

Something or someone had got through to Harry. He was having fun, which she had always believed education should be but rarely was.

Before she replied, she decided she must find out a little more about Macbeth and look at Banquo and Duncan in depth. Until then her knowledge of the play had been clouded by the image of the school production in which the part of Lady Macbeth was taken by an extremely pushy, unpleasant girl who had bullied others and had an overdeveloped sense of her acting ability, a sort of female Laurence Olivier. There had been a great deal of wringing of hands and the girl made the most of 'out damned spot', but Julia doubted whether she had a conscience. It was rumoured that her parents had given a large donation in the form of a scholarship for her to get the part. It was clever casting by the school.

There must be a *Complete Works of Shakespeare* in the house somewhere; better still, one of those slim volumes of plot cribs which saved you from reading the whole thing.

She found a complete works covered in dust in the dining room and settled down to familiarise herself again with the bard. She had done *Twelfth Night* for the School Certificate and got a credit. She remembered writing something about feeling sorry for Malvolio, who was picked on.

In her reply to Harry she must get it right; this might be her last chance to keep his mind from brooding about injustice and divert it into a thirst for knowledge.

As she blew the dust from the pages, she heard her mother's voice shouting 'go and look it up' and saw again the library of her old home, that great edifice, the privileged rural sanctuary of her youth. During most of her childhood it had not been used as a library but as a wartime nursery. Its shelves were still laden with rows of battered dark blue pictorial encyclopaedias almost too heavy for small hands to lift.

She remembered those encyclopaedias with deep affection. They had a musty smell and some pages were stuck together by sticky fingers. They were not only used to look things up, but piled one upon the other to become part of the fortifications in games of cowboys and Indians. When the old nursery upright piano lost one of its casters, Volume M–N was wedged beneath it.

She remembered pulling at a heavy volume, letting its weight thud to the floor, turning the tissue-thin pages holding their cornucopia of things unheard of, until you found what you were looking for. Being side-tracked and tempted by other words. Mother really understood education.

Julia felt sorry for Harry. He had loved reading as a small child when his imagination was allowed to let rip but since the court case he had been seduced and groomed by a new technology. He found solace in what Matt called that 'clever devil's instrument', believing that within it could be found the whole of life's experience. Harry stroked his smartphone continually to find a new thrill, its images so transient and shallow that he had to move on to the next picture or message for reassurance. He had lost his trust in people.

The summer after the court case, there was the Malaga incident. Harry had already decided that school was the very worst place to try and learn, and a colossal waste of time and of his life. Then something unexpected came up. Sitting Spanish at GCSE because it was easier than French, Harry had been chosen to go on an exchange school visit to Spain. The offer had been greeted with such high hopes; a trip abroad was one of the few perks of education which might have some practical or long-lasting benefit.

Gosh, Granny, I'm so excited. I haven't been abroad before and, like Dad, I've never been in an aeroplane. There are twenty of us going to somewhere called the Basque country, to a school in Bilbao. My exchange is with a girl called Valentina. I talk to her on Facebook. She sent me a photo and she's very pretty. Tom and Chris say I get all the luck. I haven't shown the photo to Sophie, she might not understand. Did I tell you about Sophie? We are in a Facebook relationship.

Valentina's family have kindly invited me to stay on an extra

week and go with them to their apartment in Malaga. I sent
Valentina photos of the farm, and one of Pearl, Mum's mare,
with her new foal and V sent me a photo of her dog having
a shampoo at a dog's beauty parlour with a note saying how
she already loved the foal, absolutely cute, can't wait to hug it,
I absolutely LOVE animals and can't wait to be with you –
thanks for agreeing to be my exchange. Gran sorry I forgot to
say that V is brilliant at languages, she already speaks German,
English and French and is learning Mandarin. Dad says he
hopes she has common sense.

Julia's first reaction to all this was: is the Basque country safe? Were all those ETA separatists still blowing up things? If anything happened to Harry and she had encouraged him to go, she wouldn't be able to live with herself.

When the first messages arrived they were encouraging. *Love Spain, Granny, it's lovely and hot.* He appeared to be getting on well with Valentina's parents. The mother taught IT at the local college and the father was something high up in local government. From what Harry had told Anna, they seemed to be rather wealthy; they had a swimming pool and lived in one of those gated prison complexes in which wealthy people now had to live. Harry sent photos on his mobile to Anna. There was a brother a little younger than Valentina. Harry was enjoying school lessons in a different environment. They had visited the Guggenheim Museum, which he described as awesome.

The first message of doubt came after four days and was sent to Julia, not his parents. *I found Valentina in tears this morning, Granny, and don't know what to do. I think her father is a control freak. Because she didn't get a top mark in some exam, he went on and on at her. It was horrible. I know*

Mum shouts at me but not like that, and although it was in Spanish I knew it was nasty.

There wasn't really anything Julia could do other than be positive. *It may be better when you get to Malaga, she replied. And the car journey south through Spain will be interesting. You may even visit Cordoba where your guitar was made.*

If she interfered, Anna would never forgive her.

But it was not better in Malaga and the journey south was uneasy. Harry wrote: *I had hoped we could stop in Cordoba where they make guitars, or Granada, but when I suggested it the father said I was being unappreciative so I just kept quiet. When we got to Malaga the apartment was tiny and I had to share a room with the brother and it was ghastly. He spent the whole time masturbating and all V wanted to do was lie on the beach in a bikini ogling other boys and making me rub oil all over her. In the end I just walked away and the father got really shirty with me. The only good thing is that the sun has made my acne a lot better. I don't know how Valentina is going to get on staying with us on the farm???!!!!!!!!!!!*

It was the first time Julia had seen word 'masturbate' in print – she hadn't even heard of it until she was twenty-five and only then in the context of it being something young boys were persuaded not to do because it could send them mad.

Julia chickened out and ignored the message. She sensed there was something else, something he was not telling her and he knew that, unlike his parents, she would never ask. She would wait until he was home again and see if he opened up, or she could ask Chloe's advice. Since her appointment as a godparent, Chloe had turned out to be a tremendous family asset. She would know about such things and Harry really liked her; they 'tweeted' together and she had become Julia's confidante as well as Harry's.

Losing his innocence and trust in such a public way on two fronts was a double whammy for Harry and Julia felt his pain. But they were such small things when weighed against the tragedies going on in the world and she had tried to explain this. He refused to listen and from that point on he became opinionated and defensive. He didn't have the knowledge and experience of life to make the right judgements but when she tried to find conciliatory words to keep him on her side, to explain a different point of view, he responded on Facebook with anger that was far harder to redeem than if it been said face to face.

Fucking, fucking fucking fucking crap, Granny and ten rows of crosses then, as an afterthought, *Philip Larkin was right, adults do fuck you up.* That was a truth Julia already accepted and she felt a twinge of delight that at least Harry was reading poetry. But greater than that delight was the use of those six words; he knew that she would understand his feelings without censure.

CHAPTER 13

Julia was well aware that she might be about to give in. The need to forget everything, to accept that nothing was important, advice given when she had suffered from debilitating, isolating depression in her forties. You could almost have given up then but now was a different ballgame. A bullying officialdom continually banged on the door of people's sanity; minds were no longer allowed to log off.

She was now in the habit of having a lie down in the middle of the afternoon. No sooner had she snuggled guiltily under the duvet than her old adversary, her bladder, awoke her and demanded her attention. What a relief, she thought, to be diagnosed by the NHS as incontinent and be allowed to let rip into a prescribed adult Pamper.

She knew she was drinking triple the fourteen units a week suggested by the nanny state but felt no guilt about that; she was saving the NHS a considerable amount by not consuming diazepam, Atarax and the other tranquilisers with which the drugs companies tempted her.

She started watching *Frazier* on Channel 4 whilst eating her breakfast muesli in bed. When Hugh was alive, he hated both. She had been denied the experience of starting the day with a good laugh and was trying to make up for it. She watched the news daily, but now Al Jazeera kept her in touch, not the BBC with its bland, parochial outpourings and its bunny-hugging attitude to animals. The Middle East was once more sending out messages of truth as it had done two thousand years ago.

Her mind was still holding on, still had a tenacity which her body had abandoned. What or whom had made living such an obstacle race? Why had life been inflicted upon anyone or anything? Who could you blame, God or Darwin? Science had eased man's physical burden but enslaved the mind. How could she get this across to Harry without sounding preachy? But she sensed that he already understood.

Poor Harry, with all his sensitivity, was going to have to go through it all again, try to make sense of creation, struggle to find the right answers, face it alone after she had gone. She remembered him saying when he was six, 'Please don't die before I'm grown up, Granny.' He had updated this only recently: 'Please, Granny, don't die before I have children, cos I want them to know you.'

She stood on the back doorstep and looked up at the sky. A strong southerly wind was bending the damson tree and in its rustling leaves she imagined she heard the words, 'I was still far off when your Son came to meet me and brought me home.' She thought she might give God and the church another go; during the trial she had neglected Him, probably due to the thought that the other side also was calling for His help. She would give the Thursday church meetings another go and hope Mrs Proudie was in South Africa visiting her daughter.

Julia's realised that the time when her drinking had got out of control coincided with a message from Harry. She had been aware over the past months that his views were becoming a little extreme, tinged with small comments about immigration, concerns Julia herself had. This sceptred isle was sinking under the pressure of too many passengers, like too many hens in a coop, starting to peck at one another.

But the message alarmed her not for its content but the knowledge that it would get him into trouble and if she queried him, he would shoot back at her about freedom of speech. She hadn't replied immediately for she was all too well aware that whisky would cloud judgement and that he had made the comment in anger, with that certainty adolescents have of believing they are right without the experience to back up their statements.

Granny, I think Enoch Powell was right. Why did people denigrate him?

And in that question Julia felt a justification for her longevity. She still might be of some use but she would need to sober up a bit first.

The whole thing was too complicated to explain and the world had changed too much from her day to be able to give an honest answer. She wondered how Hugh would have dealt with it, for he had been at the epicentre of volcanic shifts of power and influence. As one of few westerners invited into Mao's repressive Red China in the fifties, at a time when the communist regime was trying to stave off the corrupting influence of Western values, he could never have imagined that its millions of subjects would land up with the worst of both worlds: rabid capitalism and no freedom of speech.

She would need time to think.

Are you still there, Granny? You didn't answer, are you OK?
You haven't had a tumble, have you? Are you taking your stick
when you go outside? You cannot legislate or bomb other people
into loving you. Aren't the headlines horrible? It's common
sense that if you go into someone else's country and kill their
leader they are going to retaliate (is that the right word?). I
wish they had killed Blair then all this slaughter would not be
happening and I could still go hunting with Dad. It's common
sense, Granny, that if you push a stick into a hornet's nest they
will turn round and sting you. Politicians are idiots. You can't
legislate against beliefs just as you cannot teach love. What do
you think, Granny? Love you lots and lots and lots and lots and
lots and lots. The mouths of the little yellow suns were still
downturned.

Should she try and explain the Palestinian Mandate
foisted upon Britain in 1947 by the UN, the seed corn of
mistrust, that line drawn on a map which sparked off all
the recent hatred? Or should she send him, if she could
find it, that slim copy of Dylan Thomas poems selected
by Derek Mahon? Poetry might speak to him, become his
conscience and be listened to and understood better than
a history lesson.

He had responded in a small way to Philip Larkin
and Shakespeare. Perhaps putting him in touch with the
thoughts of others, finding a medium through which
she could not only express her own feelings but get her
message across, might work. Get him reading again instead
of constantly stroking that devil's instrument.

Where was it, that slither of a book with no weight
to it other than in its contents? She could see it in her
mind, had read it only recently, Thomas standing in a sepia

churchyard with that mass of curly hair just like Harry's on the cover. She searched amongst the glossy hardback irrelevancies of political biographies which she had given Hugh for Christmas then put her hand to the back of the shelf behind the carefully arranged titles and felt something soft. She pulled it out hopefully: it was an old MAAF pamphlet, dated 1960, about the control of liver fluke in sheep. She put it to one side to read later. It might be interesting to see how thing were once done.

After she had stopped looking for it, she found the small poetry book wedged as a marker in her one and only old cookery book alongside the recipe for shortbread. It was the only thing she ever baked because once upon a time someone had said how good it tasted and she had been encouraged. She read the poem again: 'The Hand that Signed the Paper'.

If she sent Harry the book she might never get it back and it would catch his attention better if she sent it online. She thought about sending it as an attachment but wasn't quite sure how to so she Facebooked the whole poem.

The hand that signed the paper felled a city;
Five sovereign fingers taxed the breath,
Doubled the globe of dead and halved a country;
These five kings did a king to death.

The mighty hand leads to a sloping shoulder,
The finger joints are cramped with chalk;
A goose's quill has put an end to murder
That put an end to talk.

The hand that signed a treaty bred a fever,
And famine grew and locusts came;
Great is the hand that holds dominion over
Man by a scribbled name.

The five kings count the dead but do not soften
The crusted wound not stroke the brow
A hand rules pity as a hand rules heaven;
Hands have no tears to flow.

Later she checked the little oblong box to see if there was a message; it was important that Harry got back to her. She needed confirmation that Dylan Thomas had reached him.

Harry's response had been immediate. *Brill, Gran, absolutely brill – thanks a lot, Gran. Gosh, how clever to capture the whole of mankind's problems in a few lines. How long ago was it written? Nothing much has changed, has it? Was Dylan Thomas Welsh like Grandpa? I hope I still have a few of his genes.*

Must rush. Sophie and me are off to the cinema to see the new Jurassic. The nerds are all signing on for the Duke of Edinburgh's awards. Mum is furious with me, has shouted at me for hours, so have put my earphones in again. I've done the bronze and silver and should have sent in the correct paperwork but forgot so won't be allowed to put it on my CV. Mum says what a waste of her time and petrol if I can't be trusted to get myself across the finishing line – she's shouting a lot these days. I think it's my GCSE results.

Julia found it quite difficult not to take sides but she knew that maintaining Harry's trust in her was paramount.

At least she had diverted his mind away from Malaga.

Harry would not slot well into his own life, let alone the expectations of others. From now on she must be on standby for the fall-out, just as she had been ready for Hugh's. Disagreements, misunderstanding and arguments, those ghastly corporate dinners when wives were assessed to see if they were up to their husbands' jobs and Hugh had set his sights on becoming a tycoon, or at the very least a business magnate. Her years of marriage to Hugh had been a good training ground for the rest of her life. It was nothing to do with the deep trust she and Hugh had felt for one another and a kind of love which rarely surfaced, other than physically. With Harry it was different: his trust and love did surface and they shared the same sense of fun, laughing at the same things, that inner giggling she had shared with her father, both realising that taking the mickey out of life was the easiest way to get through it.

There was another message waiting. Julia felt satisfaction that she had used the right bait, but now she must play the line carefully and hook gently, sensitively and slowly, haul Harry in as her father had taught her in that far-off childhood when together they fly-fished at Honeypot and Dovenby, where the Eamont joined the Eden at Rivers Meet.

Granny, the world is going quietly mad.

Was it Euripides who in 453BC had said 'Those whom the Gods wish to destroy they first drive mad'? She must play this carefully, keep his attention,

She replied: Hi there, *Harry, it's Gran again. I agree the world is going mad but not very quietly. Have you heard of a guy called Euripedes who lived in 400 and something BC?*

After she had sent it Julia realised she was adopting his form of communication, a type of jokiness; she was trying to be cool because she was unsure of herself, like those leftie teachers thinking they could gain respect by being chums with the lower sixth. Who was teaching whom?

Harry had picked up on it immediately. *Granny, the fact that the world is going mad is not funny ha ha. Do you remember asking me if I ever read a newspaper because you thought that I might find one or two articles in The Times amusing and interesting and I told you no, that I could find it all on line. I don't think you believed me. Well I took a look at that bloke Matthew Parris and you were quite right. It was about childhood – quote 'adults should value children as people'. I tried to get Mum to read it but she was too busy and said for God's sake put that thing down and listen to me.*

There was another article by the same bloke a fortnight later about forgiveness, it was brill. Did you see it – here's a quote: 'Wiping the slate clean with people who have hurt us isn't just difficult, it goes against the grain and our survival instinct.' That's how I feel about Aunt Carla and Uncle Theo. They destroyed my childhood with all that hate and the court case. I know you should try and forgive your enemy, and I try to but I can't. Being magnanimous (is that the right word, Gran?) leaves a nasty taste in my mouth. Christ said 'forgive them for they know not what they do' and I bet he meant it but Aunt Carla knew exactly what she was doing. I bet Matthew Parris listens to his children.

I scrolled some more and picked up an article by someone called Adam Sage who interviewed some guy in Paris called Michael Onfray. Did you see it? 'West has had its day, claim les miserables.' He's a temporary, sorry contemporary, French philosopher from Paris and he says the west is on the point of no return, declining under the influence of the evils of a market economy and radical Islam. Sage asked him what advice he would give the young and he replied, 'The boat is sinking. Remain elegant. Die upright.' Gosh, Granny, has it really got as bad as that? Lots and lots and lots etc. The yellow faces held a passive expression.

Julia was uncertain how to reply. Should she mention that Mathew Parris was gay and regrettably was most unlikely to have children? This message was by far the longest he had sent and she couldn't take it all in at one sitting; she appeared to have landed a salmon rather than the trout she had hoped she might net. Could Facebook messages be printed out so that she could digest it sitting in a comfortable chair?

What she needed right now was a bit of a giggle and a whisky, so she decided to postpone her reply until the evening. She would try and keep her reply light-hearted, for Harry still had to balance his own thoughts and beliefs, learn to navigate through the values of peer pressure, learn to come to terms with the anxieties and threats just as generations before had had to cope with wars and the atomic bomb hanging above their head. But now it was not only bombs but minds which were threatening and minds cannot be banned.

Before she had time to think out her reply, there was an email from Anna. *Harry is driving me to drink. He never listens to a word I say and worse still, he never tells me anything. I haven't the vaguest idea what is going on his mind. I know he talks to you on Facebook and I really resent it – why does he confide in you? You are always on his side.*

The oblong box was flashing a message from Harry. *Forgot to tell you, Granny. Valentina the exchange student is with us. Mum says she's hard work. Dad's too busy on the farm so Mum has had to do it all. All Valentina wants to do is shop and hug animals which are not used to being hugged and don't like it. She's already been kicked by the foal and bitten by one of the sheepdogs when Dad took her to see the puppies. Mum is scared stiff that she'll get tetanus.*

We took her to York. I really liked that, we walked around the old City walls which was really interesting, Mum said there is a good university there. I wouldn't mind going to university if I could live in a place like York but all V kept saying was where are the shops? So in desperation the following day Mum and me took her to the Metro Centre and she did what I saw her doing in Malaga, stealing things, putting them into her handbag. This time I challenged her, cos it would land Mum in a load of shit, and she put them back. I asked her why she did it when her parents as so wealthy and she said she couldn't be bothered to stand behind other people to pay but it got even worse.

As you know, since hunting was banned we have been plagued by foxes. They have taken all Dad's guinea fowl and we lost at least nineteen lambs at lambing. I tried to explain this to V. Anyway, Gran, as you know Dad has this great guy Steve, who takes me lamping occasionally when he comes to control the foxes. I asked V whether she wanted to come with us to see what the countryside is all about but she was too busy painting her toenails. Steve let me use his rifle – the lamp caught the eyes of the fox, it looked straight at the light, two green pinpoints. I got him fair and square between the eyes. It was an old dog fox.

I carried him into the kitchen. V was still painting her toenails and all hell let loose. She had a fit and ever since has locked herself in her room and won't come out. Mum is worrying that she may be self-harming. Everything is skewed, Granny, right has become wrong and wrong has become right.

There were times when she wished Hugh was still with her to bring some order into Harry's thoughts but perhaps it was a good thing that Hugh was no longer alive. Julia felt guilty for thinking that. His had been a cheerless upbringing and before his death he had already started to question Harry's behaviour and outspokenness, a rebellion which Hugh had almost succeeded in knocking out of Julia during their long marriage. He hadn't quite succeeded; she still possessed a streak of defiance, being 'agin the government' as mother had called it, and she had applauded her for it.

Julia needed to find someone with whom to share her worries. She had got into the habit of burdening strangers. She had become adept at cornering the men and women who delivered the mail; if she was pottering in the garden, they would say 'hard at it again' and hand her the mail with a 'nothing exciting today'. That gave her an opening, the opportunity to have a crack and still feel part of things. If they looked old enough, she would ask them if they had grandchildren and try to get some bearing on how she should react to Harry's views. But now they were always in a hurry and she had felt rejection until Anna told her that tachographs were now installed in those once reassuring red vans and passing the day was no longer allowed.

When she heard the approach of the dustcart, she waited outside the back gate hoping for a quick chat with the two nice friendly young lads, about Harry's age, who were doing 'work experience' with the recycling firm. She always tried to hide the quantity of bottles under the plastics container but she didn't fool them. They would laugh and say, 'OK, love? The garden looks good.'

That approbation from strangers got her through the day and reaffirmed her decision to turn her back on the glossy McCartney Stone brochure. She would stay put for as long as she was able, for she could still stand on the doorstep and talk to God whether He was real or unreal.

She chickened out of replying to Harry. He brought her beliefs into question. He had never been a doubter, had been certain of himself since the day he was born, whereas Julia was still procrastinating.

That Thursday Julia decided not to go to church but instead go to her study and look up the symptoms of throat cancer on the internet. She'd had this persistent cough for six months but hadn't gone to the doctor, not because she mistrusted them – she would have welcomed her input – but because deep down she believed that she really didn't matter and there was absolutely nothing wrong with her. She would rather not face that put down.

The little Facebook box was flashing, a message from Harry. *Did I tell you about Sophie? She is my girlfriend. You would like her, she laughs a lot and is very positive. She lives about five miles away so I can bike over.*

There was a PS. *Am thinking of having my ears pierced and a tattoo saying Sophie on my arm. Lots and lots and lots and lots of love, Harry.* Julia counted at least thirty little smiley yellow faces and at least twenty rows of kisses.

PPS Sorry forgot to say I am into skateboarding.

117

The comment about skateboarding gave her an opening without having to get in too deep. She had learned to resist answering emails and Facebook messages by return as she had been taught to do as a child because it was good manners, but she wrote a quickie: *Where do you skateboard?*

This had sparked a deluge of information. *I was on the bus on the dual carriageway below the castle when I got a quick flash of what looked like a person suspended in mid-air so I asked the bus driver and he said it was a skateboard park – so after school I mobiled Mum that I was doing extra revision and went to have a look.*

I asked some guy who was wearing a black tee-shirt which said 'Anarchy is cool' and a baseball cap with a skull on it whether I could have a go and he said, 'Cool man.' I really was good at it, Gran. Gonna save up and buy one. The guy taught me how to do an ollie. Please don't tell Mum any of this – she will have a hairy – I've heard her say that the park attracts weirdos and there are a lot of syringes and drug stuff lying around.

Julia was out of her depth and the need for a long pause had become essential.

Why had she not thought of Chloe before? Lovely sensible Chloe, with her down-to-earth, seen-it-all-before, underprivileged upbringing would know how to respond.

It took a long time to find Chloe's mobile number for they normally kept in touch with little written notes. Julia hoped that seeing a text from her would not alarm Chloe into thinking something was amiss. But of course, nothing alarmed Chloe.

With difficulty Julia sent a text: *Hi Chloe dear, I need advice. Harry confides in me and I must at all times keep his trust but am a little worried – as his godmother can you get back to me.*

The reply was immediate: *Don't worry, I am on Facebook with him too and he confides in me – I'll keep him on the straight and narrow. Am in Edinburgh at the moment, friends and I are doing a thing on the Fringe. Great fun – you may get a glimpse of us on TV. Will try and get Harry interested next year, he's a bit young at the moment.* How useful godparents were, loving but detached.

Julia's mind had been on fast forward for months worrying about Harry. At the same time, her body had gone into the slow motion of old age. Everything took twice as long to achieve, and her lifelong untidiness and inability to file things was now causing problems. Finding bank statements in order to fill in her income tax returns became demands upon her time and sanity, demands that did not appear to be in anyone's interest for in the end they never took anything from her.

She went obediently to have her flu jabs, prolapse ring changed, twelve-weekly B12 injections, put drops in both eyes nightly for her glaucoma. She tried to be independent and not become a burden on others or the state. She counted herself lucky that there was nothing seriously wrong with her yet.

She looked for signs of breast cancer in the mirror as the posters at the clinic insisted she must, examining her breasts intimately; although they were sagging a bit they were in quite good repair and they looked more shapely than they had in their youth when there hadn't been much for poor dear Hugh to get excited about.

Wasn't itching a sign of skin cancer? Her back itched

permanently and she remembered Hugh's back covered in benign brown extrusions the size of old pennies, which itched and fell off from time to time. No one had seen Julia's back for decades and Hugh had never been interested in it, although she had spent a good deal of time powdering and stroking his when he refused to go to the doctor. It had become a ritual in his latter days before she struggled to get him into his pyjamas before going downstairs yet again to get him his Horlicks.

She could feel the odd scabby blemish catching as she put on her vest. It wasn't really her vest but one of Hugh's which she was using up, Second World War thrift uppermost in her mind. She had two flannelette nighties in regular use which had belonged to her mother; one still bore the utility mark, those two CCs evidence of wartime quality and rationing. That Mother's flannelette nightie was still giving good service gave Julia a sense of constancy. It had survived the soaking, scrubbing, rinsing and spinning of Bosch and Zanussi and, like herself, had somehow come up trumps.

Her back was itching again; she needed something to alleviate it. Chloe mentioning the Edinburgh festival had sparked a memory: one of the children had given her a long plastic back-scratcher, a present from Scotland together with a box of Edinburgh rock after a stay with Grandpa and Step-Granny in their Queensferry flat. She remembered being relieved when the children went away, so grateful for the break. She rummaged in the attic where there was a box of keepsakes and found it. Holding it in her hand again, she wept inwardly, remembering the delight on childish faces as she accepted their present with a, 'Gosh, darlings, what a lovely thing.' It had taken half a century to come into its own.

Now she tried it out and it reached all the necessary parts. She looked at it more closely and wondered why it had appealed to childish eyes. Perhaps it was the model of a Scotsman welded onto the stem, playing the bagpipes, his kilt swirling, painted in bright brash colours.

Julia regretted that she had not made more effort to get to know her stepmother-in-law. She had been a big-boned, widowed, childless, middle-aged Scotswoman of the Clan Kerr, a daughter of the manse. It was an enormous relief to Hugh that his father had found someone to take him on in his later years. She had introduced him to classical music and they had sold the family home and moved to Edinburgh.

There were rumours in the family that in her teens she had been a suffragette and a radical left-winger, visiting Russia in the twenties, representing workers' rights, fighting against the slum conditions of the Gorbals. It was even said that she might have met Lenin, which could have been true.

Nothing daunted her. She had unintentionally embarrassed her step-grandchildren by wandering around Jenners, her large frame clothed only in a bra and a pair of huge blue bloomers elasticated below the knee, trying on hats whilst the assistant went in search of a bespoke Kerr tartan kilt for which she had come for a fitting. Even now, when Julia asked her children what they remembered about the Edinburgh festival, they all replied, 'Granny's blue knickers.'

She had never talked about the earlier part of her life

nor her first marriage. A Berlin wall was erected when she married Hugh's father, a fortress that kept out memories. She entered into her new role of stepmother and granny with concern, love, understanding and guidance.

It grieved Julia that Harry would only know her through old photographs and hearsay. How well the two of them would have got on, sharing that revolutionary streak. She would have been a stabilising influence, helping him sort out his confused forays into politics.

These thoughts assailed Julia when she was relaxing, wallowing in a bubble bath. She usually just had a good strip wash, as matron at school had called it, and submersing had become less frequent for fear of slipping and the anxiety that she would not have the strength to pull herself out of the water.

Before turning on the taps to have a bath, Julia diligently placed the anti-slip mat bought by the children into the bottom of the bath. Having failed to persuade her to install a shower, they bullied her into using the mat although the bumps on it were uncomfortable to her thinning, bony backside.

When, inevitably, she had slipped, fallen over and hit her head on the side of the bath, she cursed her stupidity. Feeling dizzy the following day, she felt it wise to make an appointment with one of the doctors for she didn't want, through her own negligence, to become a burden to her children and grandchildren. Had she not gone, they would all have chastised her.

She liked the young girl doctor, new to the practice, straight from Aberdeen University, and had not resented her first question: 'How much do you drink?'

Julia already knew that drinking habits and past misdemeanours were on line for all to see and that statistics showed that the most common cause of falling down was over indulgence. She chuckled inwardly at the thought that this pretty rookie practitioner might picture Julia wallowing in a bath with a bottle of whisky on the soap rack. Julia wished she could see her medical notes on the screen but her eyes were not strong enough.

The doctor turned from the computer and took Julia's hand. Julia felt something instinctive in her grasp, a compassion which she wasn't expecting. The doctor's hand was warm and powdery, soft like a marshmallow, and Julia wanted to hold on to it. Its touch took her back to nursery school when Miss Moore would take her hand when she was unhappy. Julia had asked, 'Miss Moore what are you going to be when you are grown up?' and the teacher had bent down, her kind face close to hers, and whispered, 'I am grown up, Julia dear.' Julia had not believed her.

Now compassion had become part of the national curriculum, a feeling to be taught. Florence Nightingale may well have been a rotten nurse, as historians wanting to make a name for themselves would now have you believe, but at least her feelings were in the right place.

Sensing that a defence strategy might be needed, Julia said, 'Someone told me that whisky thins the blood. I was made to take warfarin when I got an embolism after having my varicose veins done twenty-five years ago and thought whisky was preferable to rat poison.'

'Blood pressure normal. I wish all my patients of your age were as fit.'

And that was that; Julia's ten minutes were up and she

hadn't had a chance to say that she thought her dizziness was caused by worrying about the world and a conversation about ethics and morality might be the prescription she needed. That was ten years ago and since then she had not been near a doctor.

Now a quick word with God was all she needed. Julia stood on the sandstone flagstone at the back door and looked up at the sky above the damson tree. Two pairs of coal tits were flirting amongst its branches, pecking out the buds, showing off as spring approached, deciding who was going to go with whom. Julia felt the first warmth of the year on her skin as the sun fleetingly emerged from behind a cloud. She was thankful that the birds were taking sustenance from the tree. If they had left the buds and they had blossomed and matured into fruit, Julia knew she would have left their harvesting until it was too late. The wasps would have got there first and she would have picked the over-ripe, half-eaten fruit off the ground and felt guilty about her laziness. Better that the tits got there first; the tree didn't seem to mind either way.

The bluebottles had already emerged in the house, having spent the winter within the warmth of the curtain pelmet. They had laid their eggs, knowing that this domain was not likely to be spring cleaned. They had beaten the flycatchers. Julia had never recorded the arrival of the bluebottles but she had recorded the arrival of the flycatchers that nested annually in the clematis montana.

She heard the familiar sharp tweet-tweet of the flycatcher from an adjoining tree so she knew they were back, but their quick movements made them hard to see. Last year's nest, wedged in the crook of a branch between the bathroom downpipe and the wall, was just visible behind the opening leaves. The nest had taken a battering during a harsh winter but now she noticed that repairs were taking place; a build-up of moss, sheep's wool and downy feathers had raised its height by an inch or two.

She tentatively put two fingers to its base and felt one egg. She knew that from then on she must ignore their presence, pretend she hadn't seen them. She must also warn the postman and visitors to the back door to keep their voices down, for only eighteen inches separated the nest from the house and the constant opening and shutting of the door.

Julia tried never to catch the eye of the mother bird as she would with a human to wish them well. She lowered her eyes as she went in and out of the house so as not to threaten, fearful that the hen would desert the nest. Sometimes she cast a quick sideways glance and a tiny beak and brown feather reassured her.

By the time the eggs hatched, Julia had been accepted. The parent birds took her for granted as they carried out their shuttle service of food. And then they were gone.

Julia looked through her old diaries. The earliest recorded arrival of the flycatchers had been April 13th 2005, when instinct had told them that it was safe to leave the warmth of Africa and head for northern climes, where the dawn and dusk rises of flies and midges to feed their young would be hatching.

Chapter 14

There had been no messages from Harry for some time and Julia presumed that with his exams over he would be chilling out with friends, as he put it. When, after ten days, there was a message saying: *Granny I'm in deep shit*, she imagined the worst.

Being in deep shit when she was young had meant exactly that – up to your waist in cow muck, the squelch of slurry inside your wellies. When she was six years old, she had mistaken the hard, sun-baked crust on top of the midden as an exciting hill to be run up. She had gone through and been engulfed by a covering of shit and smell until her cries for help had been heard.

She sent a message to Harry and suggested that, as she had not seen him for months, it would be lovely if he could come and see her. She felt her time was running out and what about a sleepover? He did not reply immediately but late that evening there was another message: *Granny, may I phone you? I need to talk to someone.*

Of course, darling, you know I'm here for you any time.

She heard the phone ring almost immediately. She picked it up, tried to count to ten, determined not to panic, for Harry's mind was like an animal's and he would pick up any difference in her tone of voice.

'Hello, Harry dear?'

A chirpy female asked, 'Am I speaking with Mrs Hampton?'

Julia, caught off guard, said, 'Yes.'

The voice continued, 'And how are you today, Mrs Hampton?'

Taking the words at face value, Julia replied, 'Struggling a bit. At ninety, I'm becoming rather weary.'

She heard the dismissive digital click of commercial disinterest.

The following morning she had such good intentions; she would plan her day so as not to waste a moment for she knew she was part of the privileged old, reaching the end of a life without dementia, and should count her blessings. But until Harry rang she couldn't settle. She checked her Facebook messages; this necessity to always be in touch with him had become an obsession.

Hi, Granny – are you OK? Haven't heard from you for ages. Mum's shouting, she says are you remembering to take your bleeper with you when you go outside. Gran, what is a Hashemite? Mum and Dad haven't a clue.

Neither had Julia. It was something to do with Jordan, not the one with the breast implants but a monarchy with a king who at the moment was welcoming into his country more than his fair share of Syrian refugees. There was no mention of Harry's deep shit.

Hi, darling, something to do with Jordan. Why do you want to know?

His reply was almost immediate. *I told you about the skateboarding, didn't I? I go whenever I can cos it gives me a buzz, and there are some interesting guys. There's this black guy – well he's not really black, more dark brown, very fit, with fine features. I asked him where he came from and he said he was a Hashemite.*

Julia poured herself a large whisky and replied, passing the buck. *Suggest you look it up on the internet.*

Four days later Facebook told her there was another message; perhaps he was going to explain deep shit.

Gran, you are not going to believe this. Do you remember me telling you about this guy called Hashi? Well, he and I were skateboarding on Sunday. I went because it was pissing down and I would have the whole skateboard park to myself and Hashi turned up with the same thought. Anyway, it was a bit slippy and in the middle of a double ollie he took a bad fall and was lying there with something broken, unable to speak. I mobiled for an ambulance but after waiting fifteen minutes I rang a local taxi firm instead who came in five minutes. The driver was a Paki and helped me get Hashi into the back seat – although he did say we shouldn't be doing this, we should wait for an ambulance but I said bollocks and he agreed. We were in A&E within five minutes and I was worrying how I could pay him but fortunately had a fiver in my pocket, but the Paki wouldn't take anything.

I found Hashi's parents' number on his mobile and phoned them. Do you believe in fate, Granny, cos what happened next is amazing? Turns out Hashi's father is a neurosurgeon from Jordan, seconded for a year to the county hospital. Now they are treating me like Jesus Christ for saving their son and have asked me to join them in the summer hols in Amman where their family home is.

The following morning there was a knock on Julia's door, loud and firm. It would be her prescription from the chemist, some more Xalatan eye drops for her glaucoma. The man knew to knock loudly; the instructions on the packet said: 'Knock loudly patient very deaf'.

It wasn't the rural delivery service but a young man at least six feet tall; he had to duck to get through the door. She didn't immediately recognise him for it had been seven months since she had last seen him.

Before she could stand back and take him in, he embraced her in a long bear hug, almost knocking her off her feet. She felt on his face that first roughness of approaching adulthood.

'Hi Gran – thought I'd come and see you.' His voice was low. How, in just seven months, could he have turned into a man? She should have seen it coming, recognised that the yellow faces, rows of kisses *and lots and lots and lots and lots of love* had been replaced by t*ake care, Gran darling, my love as ever* and one or two kisses.

He was wearing a black T-shirt with a white imprint of a face she did not recognise on the front. Beneath a sleeve she thought she saw a small tattoo but pretended not to, for she knew how Anna and Matt would have already gone on about it. There was a stud in his ear and his hair was cut in an unusual style – the sides of his head shaven clean and the mass of loose conker-coloured curls that she so loved and enjoyed ruffling had disappeared, except for one long tuft standing erect on the top of his head.

She bit her tongue; she would have liked to ask him if he had heard of Samson who lost his strength when his hair was cut off. Instead she said, 'Now tell me, darling, what all the trouble is about.'

'Well, it's pretty stupid and petty, Granny. You'll probably see it in the local paper.'

Julia's heart sank; she had little respect for the press.

He continued. 'You know what a rotten summer we have had – anyway it was that very hot day and exams had finished, and what a ghastly waste of my childhood they were, Gran…'

Julia resisted the temptation to ask how he had done in the exams and thought, I'm not going to mention it. If he got three or four Bs she would send him a £20 note. She abhorred those shrieking hugging teenagers who opened there results in the presence of TV, flashing their A*s for the media, whilst those who didn't make it wandered off unseen and unheard to live a life of their own making.

'…and I was coming out of school, walking over the bridge, looking down at the water and I just decided on impulse to take all my clothes off and jump into the river. There was hardly anyone about but just as I was coming out a woman called out and told me I was a disgrace. She was taking pictures of me on her mobile, going to report me for indecent exposure and before you could say Jack Robinson, the police, social services and some bloke from health and safety were asking me my name and where I lived. Heaven knows what that little lot cost the taxpayer. The police were particularly zero chill, but you know Mum and Dad have never trusted the police. Not since that episode when Theo broke into the house and beat up Dad when I was little and Mum asked for the 999 telephone recording but the police said they had lost it.'

Julia remembered all too well, although she had tried to obliterate the memory from her mind and get back some kind of childhood trust in authority. Now mistrust was rearing its head again and she could see the headlines: 'Police give 16-year-old boy criminal record for indecent exposure'. Harry would be damned. A teenager prank done in the exuberance of youth turned into something onerous by a censorious public who now lived by double standards.

'That's not all, Gran. I'm in deep shit with Dad and I was only trying to help. I thought he would be pleased but, as you know, Gran, he is just not with it. Have you got a Coke? I walked from the station. It must be about five miles.'

Julia went into the utility room. The Coke can must have been there since Harry was little; the sell-by date was a decade old. She pointed this out but he gulped it down.

'You know what a brilliant artist Dad is. No one around here knows it and I thought what a waste of real talent so I decided to put his pictures on Twitter and appointed myself his media manager. I can put this on my CV, use it to show initiative, but then everything took off. The thing went viral and he has become a mini celeb and absolutely hates the exposure. He says I have ruined his life. That's a bit of an exaggeration really – he actually said I'd taken away his privacy. I know you took him to London but it was my idea, Granny. He was completely out of his depth. He told me he felt like a fish out of water until he chatted up the waitress who came from Bishop Auckland and whose grandfather had bought a good tup from Dad's father. It's sad, Gran. I never knew my paternal grandparents, they died before I was born – you're the only grandparent I have left.'

Julia didn't know what to say and had a strange feeling of wanting to remove herself. She changed the subject and asked him if he had given any thought to what subjects he would take at A levels.

She was pleased when he answered, 'Philosophy and ethics, psychology and Mandarin.' They were not the subjects that others thought he should take, like science and technology, which would guarantee him a place at a university and turn him into some robotic clone.

She tried to keep ahead of what was being thrown at her, at the same time wondering what to give Harry for lunch. She decided on sausage and mash with the remains of a cold chicken as a back-up.

Whilst Harry continued talking, she took an old newspaper out of the recycling bag to put the chicken bones in and saw it was a copy of *The Guardian* – it must have been left by her other son-in-law, the one who wore sandals all the time and was a bit too much of a Lib Dem do-gooder for Julia's taste.

Squinting down, she read: 'Reason must obliterate faith for the world to survive.' Typical *Guardian* guff, she thought. As usual they had got it all the wrong way round and she chortled inwardly, remembering a rather clever political joke she had heard. She repeated it to Harry; it would be interesting to know if he were sufficiently mature to see the humour in it.

'What do Charles Kennedy and Julius Caesar have in common? Answer: They were both stabbed in the back by men wearing sandals.'

Harry laughed loudly. 'I hadn't heard that one Granny

There was a pause. Harry examined a large, intricate cobweb on the kitchen window. Julia never noticed things like that nowadays and she had always admired the tenacity of spiders; you dusted them away and back they came, unfazed, and started all over again. Now she left them to get on with life and always rescued the large ones from the bath. They would be around long after mankind had disappeared, caught in its own web of profligacy and swallowed up. Spiders, Julia felt sure, understood life's necessities, adeptly cocooning and storing the surplus to be absorbed later when flies were scarce.

Harry said, 'This cobweb's just like a bit of delicate lace.' Unable to resist the temptation, he touched it lightly with the tip of his finger. The spider felt the tiny vibration and emerged quickly from its corner to see what it had caught for lunch.

Julia said, 'Don't tease it,' and added, 'Well, we could have a game trying to name different religions. I'll start: Catholics, C of E, Quakers, Baptist Methodist, Pentecostal, Islam Jehovah's Witnesses, Scientology, Buddhism, Hinduism. I think that's my lot.'

Harry immediately reeled off a list of twenty more. He said, 'The way things are going, Gran, I would put my money on Islam. I watched a guy being interviewed on TV the other day and he was brill, Iman Ibrahim Mogra, Secretary General of the Muslim Council of Britain. He had a quiet, reasoned voice and understood faith; he wasn't bogged down by ritual and all those false promises which politicians spew out at election time to get your vote and then renege on when the Whips get to them.'

Julia was floundering and wondered what conversations other grandmothers had with their grandsons. One day she would try and explain to Harry but now was not the right moment. Now she needed to know what guidance others were giving, a reassurance that she was on the right track. But there were not many of her contemporaries left; her few very close friends had long passed on, or were either in hospital recovering from broken bones after a fall or had dementia;

There must be a few acquaintances out there with late-in-the-day grandchildren who could vouch for her generation and may appreciate a telephone call from the past.

After she had run Harry to the station that evening, she made a list. She searched for couples she and Hugh had liked years ago but whose lives had taken different paths, contact maintained by the mandatory placatory Christmas card.

It must have been a surprise when a strange voice reintroduced itself as an old friend. Sometimes she had the feeling she was being passed on; a hesitant pause at the other end, then, 'I'll just get Giles.' She sensed a superficial bonhomie from someone she had once considered a friend, a falseness of tone travelling down the line. She felt it as a sniffer dog would sniff out cocaine at Heathrow.

And, of course, Hugh had been right as always. The strength of anything is in its weakest link and this could be applied to the friendship of couples. It depended whether you got on better with the husband or the wife and, in many cases, it had been their children and grandchildren who were the catalysts in the friendships.

When they were living in the south, there was a couple whom they had got to know quite well. The husband was in the navy during the war, on Artic convoys like Hugh. They met by chance outside the sports centre where their friends planned to instil discipline into their grandson, a child to whom Hugh had taken an instant dislike. His behaviour was the antithesis to the way Hugh had been brought up, to be rarely seen and unheard. This child was in your face, boisterous; he fiddled, touched and tinkered with everything. When their back was turned, he broke off one of the windscreen wipers on his grandparents' car in an effort to find out how it worked.

When they were alone Hugh said, 'I don't want that child in my house, ever.' But Julia had worked at the friendship and tried to keep in touch.

Her efforts had been thwarted by a telephone call a couple of years later. 'Hello, it's Marie. We are returning south after a lovely holiday with our grandson in Archnemuran on the A66. I know you live around here. It would be lovely to see you both again. May we pop in to say a quick hello?'

Without asking Hugh Julia had said yes, for it was in her nature and she thought it might give her a lift, but Hugh had been right. Within two minutes the grandson, Nigel, had spotted a picture on the wall, a watercolour which Hugh had commissioned of his old ship HMS *Sheffield* battling the storms of the North Sea en route to Murmansk and Archangel, taking supplies to beleaguered Russian allies. It was his most treasured possession for it held for him the comradeship of those days.

Nigel said, 'That looks like my Dad's ship.' Before anyone could stop him, he took it off the wall to have a closer look and in the process it crashed to the floor, splintering the glass.

Hugh shouted at him, calling him a blithering idiot as he did with his own grandchildren, and that put an end to what could have become a good friendship. Fifteen years had elapsed since that episode. Julia remembered they had a double-barrelled name and were rather grand. Their telephone number would be in the old address book and they were the kind of people who would not have moved house; they were mini landed gentry who would be inclined to stay put.

Feeling brave, she phoned and the wife answered. Although she'd found their grandson exasperating, Julia had liked them both and felt an immediate sense of goodwill.

'Good gracious, what a lovely surprise! Keith and I were just talking about you the other day. You will have seen on the news about Artic convoy veterans being given a medal. It's lovely to hear from you again.'

'Well, it's lovely to know you are both still going strong. What about Nigel, your grandson? What is he doing? Do you remember you popped in to see us once whilst he was staying with you when you were holidaying in Scotland?'

'How clever of you to remember Nigel's name.'

'Hugh remembered him well.'

'You said remembered. Is Hugh still with you?'

Julia had to make the inevitable explanation of Hugh's death. Then she said, 'Tell me, what is Nigel up to now?'

'Well, it's quite exciting. He did a course at the Courtauld Institute of Fine Art and got a job at Buck House, restoring porcelain and the frames of pictures with gold leaf. Very intricate and delicate work.'

Being part of the Queen's household and skateboarding in Carlisle and jumping off bridges naked were worlds apart and added to Julia's feeling of unease. She had hoped to exchange worries and find reassurance. Of course, Nigel had had a head start; older than Harry, he had escaped Twitter, Instagram and the narcissism of selfies.

The following day, an ominous black cloud hung in the sky to the east. Julia had planned to spend time in the garden, find some peace of mind deadheading the roses, persuading them into giving her a late flowering. She wanted to escape the distressing news that ISIS had destroyed the Temple of Baal Shamin in Palmyra, where she had stood as a solitary tourist on one of her many solo travels. Hugh had refused to go with her saying, 'Tourism had become the haves gawping at the have nots'. But her night spent in a Bedouin tent in the desert had convinced her that Hugh was wrong, for the have nots had everything and the gawpers had nothing of real value.

Gardening was becoming a challenge. She needed to hold onto her stick to keep her balance because of her unreliable knee joints. She knew she was vulnerable. She clambered to the back of the herbaceous border to prune the climbers on the wall. When she hooked the high ones with the crook of her stick, she lost her balance and fell.

There was an unexpected clap of thunder followed by the staccato of giant hailstones. She had left her bleeper on the kitchen table. She lay there, cold, cursing her stupidity, as always angry with herself. The isolation of her home, which had always given her such contentment, was beginning to have its drawbacks. But she had got out of tricky situations before. She lay there thinking, in the hands of the elements as she had been all her life. They were honest, they understood her strength just as she understood theirs. Had the wind ever been given a gender in mythology? Her mind was wandering a bit.

A branch of a shrub had bruised her cheek and her head had hit something hard but there were no bones broken. To get to her feet before the cold got to her, she needed something firm to hold on to. If she could push and slither her way forward it was there: the garden seat. It had arrived, pristine, fifty years ago; solid polished oak with a guarantee from the manufacturers. It was a present from their children on their silver wedding anniversary. Like her, it had become sun bleached, hardened, gnarled and greyed by time but it still had a will and determination to survive, its strength intact.

She felt the coldness of the hailstones beneath her hand and knew she must make an effort to reach it. Harry still needed her and she had never told him how once she had slept in a Bedouin tent. Without her, who would teach him the rules by which he would be made to live? He was vulnerable, still living by the old rules which made him a target.

She was almost there. One more heave and her hand grasped the arm of the seat; she slowly pulled herself up, using every fibre of her strength, and sat on the seat breathless amongst the decomposing leaves, bird droppings and exquisite pinkish snail shells. For the first time she noted the beauty of the silver-grey lichen which covered the seat, each one different in size and intricacy like miniature lacy doilies. She ran her fingers over them; they were rock hard and had been absorbed by their host.

She glanced at her watch and tried to remember what day it was. She was confused by the fall and felt an overwhelming desire to go to church but was uncertain why. She must in some way ensure that she would still be there for Harry, and prayer might be a good start.

It must be Thursday, for she could remember putting out the waste paper. It had been so full of junk mail that she had had to drag it step by step across the cobbles and afterwards felt exhausted. If she hurried, she could make the morning half-hour service of readings and the Eucharist. She would risk Mrs Proudie.

She brushed the loose mud from her jacket, washed her hands and, still wearing her gardening jeans with a hole in one knee, half ran across the two fields to reach the isolated church. She sat in her usual pew, half way up on the right directly under the overhead electric heater. Thankfully it was on and she would dry out. Church coffers were sparse and the PCC had been economising on heating; perhaps the hailstones had been the deciding factor. She couldn't see Mrs Proudie.

She heard the click of the heavy latch on the studded Norman door: a latecomer. He sat down in the pew in front. It was Mr Proudie, without his wife. Of course he wasn't really Mr Proudie, he was His Honour Judge Hughes. Julia tried hard to concentrate on the prayers but the reading of the Gospel, a reading from Ephesians all about evil, had totally upscuttled her thoughts.

On one of her solo travels she had climbed to the top of the huge Roman amphitheatre in Ephesus to find its highest place, to get a feel of how it must have been to be on the receiving end of one of Paul's epistles. His audience hadn't exactly been over the moon about what he was trying to warn them against and had practically run him out of town.

On the day that she was there, a group of loud-mouthed Americans tourists were trying out the acoustics, raucously shouting to try and get an echo, interested only in the now and not the then. How long would it be until ISIS reached Ephesus?

Julia should have been concentrating for prayers were being said on her behalf for the whole world but she couldn't hear because, as usual, the hearing loop wasn't working and her mind was somewhere else. So absorbed was she in the warm sun of Ephesus that she completely missed standing for the Collect, and the Peace came upon her unexpectedly.

Mr Proudie turned to her and, clutching her hand in both of his with genuine warmth, looked her in the eye and said, 'Peace be with you.'

Julia replied, 'Peace be with you.'

She would stay behind for coffee and biscuits and try and have a word. He might know what to do about Harry and she had never really had a chance to talk to him, for Mrs. P always dominated the conversation whilst he pretended to re-examine the triptych. Julia wondered whether that was why he had become a judge: not being able to get a word in edgeways at home, he could now hold his own court.

After the Blessing he turned round again and she said, 'Your wife is not with you today. I hope all is well and she hasn't got this nasty bug which is going the rounds.'

'No, no, she's in South Africa visiting our daughter and son-in-law and grandchildren.'

Here was an opening; they could discuss grandchildren and bring Harry's problem into the conversation.

Leaning towards her he said, 'Excuse me, may I?' and

removed a leaf from her hair.

She walked contentedly home across the fields, feeling she had successfully unloaded her concerns for Harry upon someone who understood. It was only when she was within two hundred yards that she saw the flashing lights of a police car outside her gate. When she got nearer she saw two police vans and four policemen in bright yellow reflective jackets. She panicked and started to run; she must have left her electric blanket on and the house was on fire, or someone had broken in.

She hastened her steps. The field she was crossing seemed bigger than usual, her legs heavy just as they were in those worry dreams when you are in a hurry and your legs become leaden. Anxiety was making her breathless. Something truly awful must have happened to warrant such a large police presence.

It was then that she saw Fred and his mate Cliff, who delivered fresh fish every first Thursday of the month, nonchalantly smoking cigarettes and chatting to the police. She hoped they were not in any trouble; they were lovely guys. They enjoyed coming to her for the good crack, a mug of coffee and a bit of reminiscing and putting the world back to where once upon a time it had felt good. They went up ladders for her and reached down heavy things from top shelves, went into the loft searching for something she was convinced was up there and hadn't seen for thirty years.

Their white van was wedged between the two police vans in one of those pincer movements she had watched on *Cops Reloaded* on daytime TV; it all seemed out of place in a rural lane.

She must be careful not to appear to be some batty

old busybody, not allow her curiosity to show, so she said, 'Good morning. Pleased to see that hailstorm has blown over.'

'Morning, ma'am.' It was a long time since she had been called that.

Sensing that all was amicable, she called to Fred as though the police weren't there. 'Did you knock on the door, Fred? Sorry, I just popped down to the church. Have you any fresh plaice?' Fresh plaice was a habit; Hugh had loved it covered in egg and breadcrumbs. Prepared and wrapped in plastic had not been to his taste, so fresh plaice it had always been, and that was why Julia had taken such a shine to Fred and Cliff, who delivered it from Whitley Bay.

The port on the north-east coast held other memories. In the 1940s, one of Hugh's uncles owned a fleet of trawlers and had lived in Monkseaton. Because of his age he had been turned down for active service in the Second World War so he joined the ARP. Because of his influence in the town, he was put in charge of a concrete pill box with its own searchlight and ack-ack gun. He had turned the pill box into a men's nightclub, complete with bar, portable cooking stove and easy chairs, where his buddies could meet to escape their wives for the night with a genuine excuse, and occasionally take a blast at an enemy plane which had lost its way on its return from bombing Glasgow.

Because Hugh had told this tale many, many times, Julia felt she knew Whitely Bay well and the strong Geordie accents were reassuring. From time to time Fred called her 'bonnie lass', 'petal' or 'flower', which was lovely and made her feel young again.

She tentatively approached one of the policemen to

ask what the trouble was. An outsider, a second-home owner in a neighbouring village four miles away with no understanding of how things were done in rural communities, had reported Fred and Cliff to the police for illegal trading. The police, obliged by the law, had notified Trading Standards and, because of the fish, the Health and Safety Executive. Their offices were located in Kendal, forty miles away, and the four policemen, Fred, Cliff and now Julia were awaiting another layer of officialdom. Estimated time of arrival about forty minutes.

As it had started to hail again, Julia suggested they all come in for a cup of coffee.

When Julia was little, the village bobby was always invited into the drawing room for a drink at Christmas with the family; during the week he had a cup of tea in the kitchen if he was passing. She knew things were different now and she noticed the police hesitate; perhaps the manual on community policing didn't cover hospitality and good will. She said, 'I don't want to get you into any trouble'

The older policeman said, 'What the hell.'

As they gathered around the table the young one, who looked about Harry's age, said, 'You may not remember me. I sat at this table a few years ago when your husband died.'

She looked at him more closely and saw again the young boy in a smart uniform smelling of newness who had put his arms about her and comforted her as she wept and showed him Hugh's body sprawled across the kitchen table.

She had rung 999 because, although he was ninety-one, somehow Hugh's death had been unexpected. She had never imaged that the day might come and she wept uncontrollably at the suddenness of it all. They would never talk again, never have a chance to put right their differences and say the kind words they were both capable of, and now the guilt set in. If she had taken the trouble to go on one of those government sponsored first-aid courses, she might have been able to revive him.

This bobby had held her in his arms and comforted her, stroked her greasy unwashed, thinning hair with compassion. She smelt again the freshness of his aftershave. Hugh had never used aftershave.

She said, 'Yes, yes, I do remember you. You were so kind and told me what I must do – please remind me of your name.'

'Bowie.'

'Like the…'

She hadn't time to finish before he replied, 'The singer, yes.'

They both laughed.

The trading officer arrived in due course, followed ten minutes later by Health and Safety. The hilarity of the situation was lost on them. They were officials of the new school and had no concept of the Kafkaesque situation in which they were participating. Particulars were taken and all appeared above board; Fred and Cliff's licence to trade was valid. Goodbyes were said and Julia hoped young Bowie wouldn't be part of the police cuts.

CHAPTER 15

That the seeds of Julia's anxiety had not fallen upon stony ground became apparent when the case against Harry had been dropped, although Harry emerging naked and dripping onto the dual carriageway had already gone viral on the Internet. He appeared unfazed and 'deep shit' had faded into the background.

Julia felt she should thank someone; she was unsure whether it had been divine intervention or Mr Proudie. Perhaps a quick telephone call or one of those little thank-you cards, but that might be inappropriate; it could re-emerge decades later and compromise him or his family.

She would go to church again in two weeks' time and, if Mr Proudie were there, give his hand an extra squeeze and look him in the eye during the Peace. That, she thought, was the safest option for she couldn't get it wrong.

She must try and be more assertive about these small decisions which were beginning to overwhelm her. Assertion had never fitted her well, never suited her and if it ever had she had grown out of it or it had shrunk in the washing machine of life.

She now longed for that veteran self-confidence which all her remaining contemporaries seemed to possess. Her right to continue existing needed to be confirmed. She recognised that it was in the trivial day-to-day actions and encounters with others that it would be found, not cocooned on a world cruise amongst strangers. That kind young bobby and the encounter with the fish sellers had been a start.

Only that morning she had been on the receiving end of an octogenarian seeking a purpose and, in a way, it had come about by having fallen in the herbaceous border.

Because her face still bore a heavy, yellowing bruise below the eye, she had postponed her weekly visit to the supermarket. She was sure that Lorraine at the checkout, with whom she was fairly intimate, would say, 'Had a bit of a ding-dong with hubby, have you?' In the north, the real north above a line drawn between Lancaster and York, you were still allowed to say such things without giving offence. Lorraine would have forgotten about Hugh's death six years previously.

Normally Julia went on Mondays when the car park was not a challenge but she had left it until Friday, hoping the bruise would subside. But winter had arrived overnight, a covering of snow making the roads deathly icy. She had lived with these changes of the elements all her life and felt a rapport with them. She walked carefully with her stick across the cobbled yard, tested the slipperiness of the lane and decided to chance it.

The supermarket car park was almost empty. As she turned off the ignition, there was a knock on her window and a man's hooded face stared at her through the frozen glass. Her immediate thought was that it was an animal rights activist, for she still had the remnants of a green and red sticker on the rear window saying 'Keep Hunting' which had been there for over a decade. In the past it had been the recipient of two fingers and a snarl from a balaclava-clad head but now it usually got a thumbs up from a passing lorry driver and a toot on a horn.

She wound down the window to see a smiling man in a bobble hat. 'Thought I should warn you, I went a purler. It's like an ice rink. I'll wait and you can take my arm.'

Julia wept inwardly for his kindness. It took her a while to disentangle her knees and she apologised for keeping him waiting. Still seated in the car, she tentatively placed a foot on the ice and it slipped beneath her weight. 'Gosh, you are right. How very kind of you.'

'Take your time.'

'We may both go down together.' They laughed.

She asked his name and where he lived as they slithered their way to the covered trolley park, their arms tight against one another. As she put her token in, she said, 'You're a good Samaritan. Thank you so much.'

'See you around.'

She returned home with an overwhelming sense of wellbeing. Before she started to unload the car, she turned on the kitchen radio and poured herself a treble whisky.

Handel's Messiah. As the crescendo of alleluias reached its climax, she thought she was about to have an orgasm but, never having experienced one, was unsure what to expect. She had read about such things in the magazine section of the Saturday *Times* when celebs had been happy to offload their physical highs and make readers feel they had missed out on something.

Julia thought she must have been a bit of a disappointment for Hugh, although he had never said anything nor complained. She had been quite happy to accept the sex on offer but, between those bouts of pleasurable physical acts, she had found it difficult to deal with his regular verbal unkindness when they had nothing left to talk about.

Since her fall she had avoided Facebook conversations with Harry. It was important that they were always honest with one another. He always asked her how she was and if she told an untruth it might come back to haunt her. If she mentioned the fall, the children would start bullying, tempting her into McCarthy Stone or, even worse, a Bupa care home.

Because her computer was getting old, she now kept it on all the time because if she turned it off it took a long time to warm up. She felt sympathy with it, for it was hanging on to its usefulness just as she was, gasping for breath.

She checked her emails: nothing. She clicked onto Facebook and there was a message from Harry. With a mixture of dread and pleasant anticipation, she opened it.

Hi Granny. You remember I told you about Sophie and how I was in a relationship with her? I posted it on Facebook in May, you may have seen it.

Julia vaguely remembered something of the sort, that he had got a girlfriend, whom Anna had assured her was a good influence; the girl played hockey, junior team for the county and wasn't into sex, drugs or heavy metal. At the time Julia wondered exactly what the word 'relationship' on Facebook meant. What did it signify? A relationship between a seventeen-year-old boy and a fourteen-year-old girl; was it even legal? Or would the tabloid press or a recently elected wet-behind-the-ears back bencher ask questions in Parliament and turn it into something else?

Her eyes were still fixed to the screen.

I don't know what to do, Gran. I like Sophie, she's really nice and I felt a buzz that I had got a girlfriend and put it on Facebook and it made me feel good. She was someone to talk to, like a sister.

Even Anna accepted that Harry being an only child was not a good thing. He had no one other than his parents to bounce things off and they never really listened. Perhaps that was a little unfair on Matt; he did his best but he, like Julia, was floundering in a world he no longer understood. Matt was still in the garden of Eden, trying to defy the serpent, still of the opinion that the meek would eventually inherit the earth. Like the Dalai Lama, he maintained a childish innocence that perhaps the world would one day be, or could be made, a better place. That was a dream Julia had long since abandoned; she made an effort to stay light-hearted about it and had developed a kind of octogenarian jokiness to disguise her disappointment that things were not going to turn out for the best.

But she won't stop texting me, Granny, and its doing my mind. She texted me forty times yesterday and then late at night sexted me with a selfie of herself with nothing on. I told her it was a silly thing to do but she just texted ha ha ha and said I was a wimp. I said I couldn't take it any more – I thought I loved her, Granny, but it was not in the way I love you. Now she's gone off in a huff and says she got a new boyfriend. My friends say she's just winding me up and I am well rid of her.

Julia was stuck in the middle and she didn't want to be there; if her parents had understood contraception probably she wouldn't have been. She also felt sorry for Sophie, who would by now be feeling shame, wishing she had not been so stupid and hoping Harry had not downloaded her selfie or shown it to his friends.

She knew that she must get her reply to Harry right; that this might be a last chance. If she didn't, there would be a third denial at a later date. She saw again St Peter's tortured guilty, sad face on the icon in the monastery of St Catherine in Sinai which she had once visited, solo, without Hugh who in those days saw the Middle East only as a business opportunity to be plundered.

Julia's interest had been fired by an eighteenth-century engraving she had seen in one of the old encyclopaedias. She felt the need to go and see it for herself and perhaps fit in a visit to the ancient red-rose city of Petra at the same time, for she had always had a fascination with the Nabateans and their ability to find water in the middle of that mountainous arid desert region.

She had contacted the British consulate in Aquaba, for it was a time before tourist agencies included such places in their itineraries. Travel was still travelling, and you could cross from Jordan into Egypt and back again without a strip search. The consulate had been extremely helpful and arranged for a car-owning Bedouin to be at her disposal and act as her guide. Would she mind sharing this transport with a like-minded Dutch man who had made a similar request?

So it was that she had found herself sitting in a rusty, low-sprung old bull-nosed Morris, just like the one father had owned in the thirties. She could still remember its number plate, BRM 777. It was the car Mother drove to that tiresome and best-forgotten final seaside holiday in

1939, the year that changed everything.

Julia wondered how on earth this car had arrived in the desert. Perhaps it had been shipped out to Jordan to satisfy the dreams of some bored underling in the consulate and in its final years been acquired by her Bedouin and found a new home.

The portly Dutchman, who spoke not a word of English, had, on seeing the back seat piled high from floor to roof with cans of petrol leaving little space for a passenger, bagged the front seat.

He was dressed immaculately in a pale linen suit and Panama hat. He reminded Julia of Peter Ustinov's unconvincing portrayal of Poirot in *Murder on the Nile*, without the moustache.

In a way it was a good thing that language prevented conversation. Julia felt that he, like her, wanted to be alone; like her, he had compromised out of necessity to experience a dream. It confirmed her belief that you must never judge anyone by their outward appearance for it was irrelevant to what was going on their minds.

The journey had taken ten hours; Julia vomited from car sickness, the overwhelming heat and smell of petrol fumes. They had stopped once at a Bedouin encampment and been offered green tea and a spicy goat stew. After that they stopped once or twice only to relieve themselves and refuel the car. They arrived after sunset and slept in the car until awakened by Yusaff who, with a torch in his hand, indicated that they must follow him.

They climbed in silence to reach the top of Mount Sinai, breathless and stumbling, for what seemed an eternity. There they stood in the place where God had spoken to

Moses to witness the coming of the dawn. She had felt a cleansing but was unsure from what she had been cleansed; she wondered if the Dutchman had been searching for the same thing.

Now Julia was weeping for that lost innocence and the thought that Harry might not get a chance to experience, nor share, that sense of awe as she watched the huge orange red sun rise over the desert horizon of nothingness. Now the Foreign Office had advised tourists not to go there. ISIS could be hiding behind the Burning Bush and the desert had lost its virginity to the detritus of an invasive alien civilisation. Now the sandstorms carried evidence of a western presence: empty plastic water bottles and plastic wrappers, the wind creating great rubbish dumps of profligacy.

She must not make the same mistake of a wrong reply like the one she had given Harry all those years ago as his small, strong voice fought against the wind on the summit of Gowbarrow and she picked up his distant muffled question, 'Am I in heaven, Granny?' and she had said no.

The brightness of the computer screen brought her down to earth.

Well, Harry darling, there is a difference between being in love with someone and loving someone unconditionally.

She wondered what sort of sex education he had received from Matt, for there had been that incident at primary school when Harry was six. His father had asked Harry what he had learnt at school that day and the boy had replied, 'We learnt how to put a condom on a cucumber.' Matt had stormed into the school the following morning and shouted at the headmistress. 'You should be teaching children how to grow cucumbers not using them as a sex objects.'

Mrs Blenkinsop replied, 'It's part of the government's curriculum.'

Matt, who had left school at the age of fourteen, felt defeated. For the remainder of his time at primary school Harry became the victim of his father's concern and Mrs Blenkinsop's vindictiveness.

This episode, in no small part, had shaped what Harry had become – and of course he carried Julia's genes of dissent. Julia's mother had interpreted her stroppiness as being 'agin the government'; Father had called it 'Bolshie'; those who had attempted to educate her called her 'lazy and stubborn', and her brothers said she was 'pig-headed'. Her dear godfather Nunky had called it being 'a thinker and a radical', but now if you became a radical the media automatically branded you a terrorist.

What is unconditional love, Gran?

She had to get this right: 'Well, it's sort of being content with what you have landed up with,' didn't sound quite right.

Well, it is the feeling that you cannot bear not to be with someone, however annoying they are, and it has absolutely nothing to do with wanting to have sex with them. Julia thought that would do it for the time being. She wondered whether to tell him about the one real love of her life which had miraculously happened in her twilight years. Would he understand or see it as sordid, a betrayal of his grandfather? Would it belittle her in his eyes? She would leave it for now but one day she would tell him.

Harry's Facebook message continued: *I am struggling a*

bit with A levels and have probably chosen the wrong subjects. I think the headmaster is a fascist. Did I tell you I was nearly expelled because of my haircut? What the hell does that matter when millions of refugees are being driven from their homelands and climate change has flooded the county again? Hell, Gran, I don't want to grow up. Remember me telling you about that French philosopher bloke? He was right.

Julia had just read a disturbing article in *The Times* about the prevalence of depression in teenage boys and worried about Harry, for she had suffered depression herself and it was a hell she never wished to revisit or wish on anyone, friend nor foe.

He must have sensed her concern. *Don't worry about me, Gran, I'm fine. It's just that things are not turning out as I expected. I was chosen for the school rugby team to visit Philadelphia and I was really excited about it, but now it has been cancelled because of a terrorist threat, just as Dad had reluctantly agreed to cough up the money for the air fare. Typically, the school has got cold feet but I'm not giving up.*

Do you remember I told you about Hashi? I met him skateboarding. He is Jordanian, his father is a well-known surgeon in Jordan and had been seconded to the local hospital here. We keep in touch. The family have returned to Jordan and Hashi's father now works for Médecins sans Frontières and is based in the Al-Mowasah Hospital. They have invited me to Amman and I have got a job as a waiter to pay for the trip and am going in the summer hols, whatever Mum and Dad say. They are having kittens and say it's a war zone and look what happened to those tourists in Sharm el Sheik. They don't seem to understand that I'm not going as a tourist, Granny, I'm going to be with real people. I'm seventeen and I've got my passport

154

so am going whatever they say. Please, please, please will you back me up?

He pleaded knowing that she would. He possessed that certainty of himself which she had never had, that certainty which makes trust irrelevant. His hosts might take him to Petra, something she always dreamt of doing with him one day. She also knew that if it all went pear-shaped she would, for the remainder of her life, bear the consequences.

It took a lot of persuading to convince Anna and Matt to let him go until Julia pointed out that he already possessed a passport and they couldn't really stop him. Surely it was better that he went with their blessing.

Letters and emails were exchanged, assurances given by Hashi's family and trust established. Harry promised to return to sit his A levels and sent a message: *Will Facebook you when I arrive in Amman. Don't worry, Gran darling, Hashi's parents will be there to meet me. I am certain that this will be far more interesting than revising for A levels. Gran, darling, you are a star, big big hugs and lots of smiley yellow faces.*

Julia didn't feel like a star, she felt like a traitor, but she also knew that it was a question of loyalty and trust and these two had always been in conflict.

She need not have worried; once upon a time she had been concerned that Harry was too much in thrall to his smartphone but now he was its master and it was obediently communicating with her ageing computer.

This place is awesome. Hashi's father says their neighbours, Iraq, Syria and Iran, are oil-rich. Jordan has none but they have something far more precious – Petra and Mount Nebo. They are a super family – Hashi has two elder sisters. They didn't come to Britain because they're at university reading medicine. I know this is an unkind thing to say but the best thing that has ever happened to me was Hashi breaking his leg skateboarding otherwise I would not be here. Do you believe in fate, Granny?

Hashi's dad is taking us north to one of the Syrian refugee camps at Zaatari just east of a town called Mafray where he works – look it up on a map, Gran. He wants me to observe the results of war. He never lectures me, just shows me and lets me make my own assumptions. I really love this family. They are Sunni Muslims and I want to stay in this country forever but I promised you that I would come back and sit my A levels which I will do. You'd call it hedging my bets – an insurance premium to be paid towards the uncertainties of life.

In that message she knew he was subjugating what he really wanted to please her and, in that instant, Julia knew he had reached adulthood. It had taken him seventeen years whereas Julia, at eighty-nine, hadn't got there yet.

The following year he took his A levels and was offered a place at Cambridge.

For his gap year he returned to Jordan and never came back.

CHAPTER 16

Because of her declining years Julia's felt his absence like a bereavement – she might never see him again. But he was still on Facebook and she still having to act as 'go between'.

Gran, darling, try and explain things to Mum and Dad, I think Mum understands but me getting into Cambridge meant such a lot to her and I know she thinks I am throwing my future away. Dad cannot understand why I don't want to be a farmer but he has known that since the day I was born. He keeps reminding me that I am the fifth generation to own the land, which makes me feel guilty. I know I must be a bit of a disappointment to him, for he always dreamt of me working alongside him. Perhaps one day I may return to manage it. He listens to you, Gran. Could you persuade him to employ a Polish worker to take on some of the hard labour? I would hate him to sell up. I think they both feel betrayed but I really feel needed and valued here.

He was feeling Julia's guilt.

It was a letter from Hashi's father to Matt and Anna, explaining what had happened, that clinched it.

Harry's visit to the refugee camps at Zaatari had made a deep impression on him and he had asked what he could do to help. He's been working alongside UNICEF doing menial jobs during his gap year. What he really wants to do is study medicine. Because he fluffed his science GCSEs this is impossible in the UK. Because of his Cambridge success and my deep respect for your son, the medical school in Amman, on my recommendation, would be prepared to offer him a place to read medicine but it will be a long hard road for him.

So it was that the decision was made but Julia had sensed that there was more to it than that. Her suspicions were confirmed when, a year later, Harry had Facebooked her to say: *Do you remember me once asking you about love? Well, I have met this wonderful person. She's a bit older than me, a junior doctor in the hospital. Her name is Abrinet, which in Ethiopian means 'she emanates light' which she does. Her parents moved to Jordan before she was born and she is an orthodox Tewahedo Christian, but it doesn't matter about religion. All you need is faith. You will love her, Granny. She's tall, slim, kind and beautiful and is teaching me Arabic.*

I've told Mum and Dad about her and Dad says years ago he met a beautiful Indian girl on the A69 but never saw her again. He never mentioned it to Mum. Poor old Dad, I have a feeling he doesn't know the difference between an Indian and an Ethiopian, but he's pretty good on breeds of sheep.

I have been studying hard and Abrinet is an enormous help. The Arabic is coming on well and I can just about make myself understood socially. The medical side is more difficult.

Last week we went to Petra. Abrinet has been many times before. It is the most awe-inspiring place, a hidden city in the middle of the desert, hewn out of rock by the Nabateans. Abrinet says they were the most gifted people of the ancient world. It has become a bit touristy. Most people don't get beyond the Siq and al Khazneh but Abri has known every inch of it since her childhood when there were no tourists, only Bedoiuns living

158

in the caves. For an hour we climbed up what seemed to be a
rock face, Abrinet racing ahead, jumping from rock to rock like
a surefooted feral goat and we reached a tiny plateau and the
monastery of Jadal ad-Deir. The only human presence was an
aged Bedouin with an even older donkey, laden with water
carriers. Abrinet spoke with him in his dialect – he has lived
there all his life in a cave. I think he had the real measure of
life. How did the Natabeans do it? They constructed a whole
water system for that great arid city, channelling underground
streams. How on earth did they know where water could be
found in that vast desert? We stood there for hours just looking.

Abrinet said, 'Such beauty and nothingness surrounded
by mayhem, hatred and violence.' And believe me, Gran, it
is mayhem. There's so little our team can do about it – you
will have seen all the graphic details on the newsreels but
nothing prepares you for the desperate sadness, resilience and
resignation of the women. They retain their dignity under the
most appalling conditions. The children feel it less than the
adults for they have known little else.

To change the subject, the rocks are a type of red sandstone,
beautiful, like the sandstone of the Eden Valley. Do you
remember taking me to Lacy's Caves – strata of shades,
terracotta, pinks and blue?

Julia was certain that somewhere in the attic there was
a small glass dome filled with different layers of coloured
sand but it said 'a present from Scarborough'.

She thought the message from Harry had finished, but
there was a blank space where normally he would send his
love and kisses. She was about to turn off Facebook but
inadvertently scrolled down and encountered row upon
row of yellow smiley faces. There was another message:

Gran, I absolutely adore Abrinet. I cannot bear to be separated from her I am going to ask her to marry me. I know Dad and Mum will have a fit – she is eight years older than me but in this country age doesn't matter.

Julia, who had perhaps had too many whiskies far too early, wrote: *Go for it* and without a second's thought clicked send.

She had not known, but may have suspected, that this was her last Christmas; that was why she let it be known in a half-hearted way that she would love it if all the family, with exception of Harry, came to see her over the festive season. But they were too busy, had thought she wanted to be on her own and made commitments elsewhere.

She accepted it because she knew it was her own indecisiveness that had created the rejection. She had always told them that if she needed help she'd send an SOS and they had understood and gladly given her her own space.

Of one thing she was certain: she was determined to see another spring. On the first warm day, when the wind was gentle, she planned to walk up to the top land where Hugh lay. She would take some snowdrops for his resting place, her mobile phone fully charged as she had promised the children; the safety buzzer given her by Age Concern was of little use outside the perimeter of her garden. She needed to see once more the emerging lime-green bracken fronds, like miniature shepherds crooks, and make sure the harebells, primroses and wild gentians were still there.

Her every step needed to be planned and measured, not

left to chance; her mind, her legs and her walking stick had to synchronise or she wouldn't make it. She needed to get the timing right otherwise she might be too early in the year and nowadays she hadn't a clue what hour it was, let alone the day, week or year. If the snowdrops in the garden were out it must be February and too early for the wild primroses. She looked out of the window. The snowdrops had arrived without her noticing them, an abundance of them, more growing each year, confident of their yearly welcome – once upon a time they had been fifteenth-century Italian migrants but had bedded down, adapted, spread and enriched lives.

She never made it up to the high land. Spring brought floods, mud and winds of such ferocity that the media gave them names.

Something told her that she needed to be on the back doorstep early in the morning to watch the sun come up and at the same time have a quick word with God. Then she would go and see if Harry had Facebooked her. She stood barefoot in her nightie, her white hair wild in the cold wind, and hoped she wouldn't be spotted by the farmer foddering his sheep in the neighbouring field. He might assume something was wrong and come to her assistance when she needed to be alone.

The sun rose slowly, keeping her in suspense. It was huge and dazzling orange; she watched it until it was free of the horizon.

She returned to the house, her hands and feet numb with cold. There was a message from Harry, sent the previous evening. *Hi, Gran darling, I am standing on our balcony with my arm around Abrinet and it feels like I have my arm around you. We are looking over the flat white roofs of Amman, watching the sun go down; this evening it is huge and bright orange. We watched it until it disappeared and I asked it to take a message to you. It will be with you by early morning.*

Her memory was really playing up, tricking her. Trivial incidents from childhood took on significance, words glimpsed briefly as she lay on her tummy in the nursery, valediction, their meaning unimportant at the time now reminding her of a sonnet by someone called Anon.

Beauty is born of sorrow. This I know...
I shall not watch the secret dawn again
Nor hear birds calling in the Summer rain
The hidden hour has fallen ... and I go
Who sought to serve and praise her here below
And she, because of old remembered pain,
Will weep and love these songs nor count them vain,
Will find in them some faint forgotten glow...

She will remember them as I commit
In this last hour myself to the unknown,
That still before her shrine the lamp I lit
Burns in the place she gave me for my own
And, sorrowing, herself replenish it,
Knowing I kneel before a greater Throne...

She had remembered every word but her memory was unsteady. Had Harry and Abrinet married two, three or four years ago, or had she just imagined it and hoped for it? Now her eyes were dim and she could no longer read his words nor take in their message accurately.

She knew that the glass of whisky in her left hand should not have been there so early in the morning. Hugh would have called it being as slewed as a newt before ten and, if ever she managed to say anything sensible, he would have said in a sarcastic kind of way, 'Is that the whisky talking?'

But circumstances had changed. Though she had loved him dearly, he was no longer there and she had to get through the remainder of her life as best she could. She lay on her bed, the comforting softness of duck down beneath her head and decided to stay there; it wasn't that she was ready to give up on life, but an overwhelming weariness had come over her.

She was in the habit of leaving the curtains open during the night so she would not miss the sky's beauty as it came and went, nor the return of the swallows, a quick flash across the window.

Some people know when the end is coming but Julia, throughout her life, had been certain of nothing. Had she suggested to Hugh that she thought she might be fading, he would have said 'rubbish', not because he didn't believe her but because he needed to deny the thought of it; her death would leave him with too many problems.

A week previously she had contacted the family again, not knowing why, and said it would be lovely to see them if they had time. She sent a Facebook message to Harry who was somewhere in Syria saying she felt tired and was going to have a day in bed. She told him not to worry. *I shall have some Scotch broth for lunch and take it up to bed in a mug with a spoon – the one you gave me for Christmas when you were little which says 'Grannies are cool'.*

163

She was about to add a 'do you remember' but checked herself; she realised he had been too young at the time. He had tugged the real pearls from around her throat, and they had scattered and disappeared through cracks in the floorboard and they had laughed together. She wondered whether the pearls would be discovered when the house was made over by new owners, keen to rip up the past. Perhaps their presence should be included in the sale details under fixtures and fittings: 'number of graduated loose real pearls under sitting-room floorboards', in the same way that it was mandatory to declare the presence of Hugh's buried body to prospective buyers of the land. Julia had never understood why this was necessary; he could no longer be troublesome.

Her mind was wandering.

She couldn't open the tin, her hands were too frail to pull back the metal tag.

She had no idea how long she lay in her bed. She had left the back door open for nothing mattered any more.

She drifted in and out of consciousness as she had done once before in her life. She was aware of her family but couldn't see them properly; they appeared to be squatting or kneeling, their heads at bed level. There were two figures standing at the end of the bed, slightly detached from the family: Matt and Chloe. She wanted to thank them for being there, and for how much their becoming part of her family had meant to her. They had helped her break away from the conditioning of her upbringing.

A small warm pulsating hand was holding hers and she lowered her eyes to see it, so black against the whiteness of the sheets, its palm pink. She felt a stubbled, unshaven cheek against hers and heard a whisper, 'This is Sentayhu, Gran, my beloved son.'

Had she imagined the words 'in whom I am well pleased'?

'A trillion trillion yellow smiley faces, Gran darling. Love you lots and lots and lots. Do you remember me letting go of your hand on Gowbarrow and racing to the top and thinking I was in Heaven? Time to let go, Gran.'

Julia tried to reply but the words wouldn't come so she obeyed, as she had all her life, and did just that. But not before her mind screamed, 'This is me, God, bloody me.'

CHAPTER 17

'Did you know that in her seventies your grandmother had a lover?' Abrinet, sitting on a cushion wrapped in Julia's old alpaca cardigan for additional warmth, rested her body against the red Aga. Harry had found instructions on how to light the Aga in a drawer in the kitchen which also contained pamphlets explaining decimalisation: how to turn ounces into grams and old recipes cut from magazines, reminders to put the rubbish out, garden secateurs, rolls of greaseproof paper, soil-encrusted rubber gloves, a hot water bottle without a stopper, pieces of garden twine, a magnifying glass a government notification from Cameron on how to vote in the 2016 referendum on which was a scribble (*Voted leave and am now feeling guilty and responsible for the ensuing chaos but a neighbour dropped in for coffee, she has three jobs on minimum wage and voted leave for the same reason and like me resents being called a racist when all we were trying to do was be honest which has made me feel better.*), an unopened bottle of Chanel No. 5 and a World War Two shell case which Harry remembered Julia using to turn off the outside tap when her hands had become too weak to give it that final resistance of certainty.

He had always admired his grandmother's untidiness, never having anything in its proper place; it was what

166

had endeared her to him and made Grandpa shout at her so much. He remembered her excitement when she unexpectedly found what she was looking for.

'Poor old Gran, how she hated the world changing. She really tried to keep up but got terribly upset by the way things were going. She voted leave in the referendum and forever after believed she had got it wrong but she was being true to herself.'

Abrinet said, 'I wished I had known her. I wish I had been with you and Sen when she died.'

'You may get to know her better than most people by reading through those scribbled notes. She used to jot down her thoughts. But whatever she may have been thinking, she was always positive with me.'

He went outside to check the oil level in the old metal tank and gave the rusty gauge a bang to make sure it was registering correctly, for he remembered Hugh his grandfather swearing at it, reaching up and hitting it with his walking stick. There was still oil in the tank.

Abrinet's pregnant belly was just beginning to show and making it more difficult for her to reach the large cardboard box of envelopes, letters, bills, memos, catalogues and bank statements wedged between her legs. Julia's scrawled, pencilled hand obliterated their initial intimations.

Abrinet felt at home in the cardigan. Harry had placed it around her shoulders, concerned that the dampness and cold of the house, which held so many memories of warmth and security for him, would feel unwelcoming. In doing so, he had smelt Julia's scent again, not a manufactured scent but the real scent of his grandmother, the sweaty outdoor scent of her which he so loved. The mustiness of a body which had lived close to the earth, unsullied by anything out of a bottle. He knew Abrinet would sense its familiarity. The cardigan's exotic Peruvian bold reds, purples and greens might remind her of a time when, as a small child, she had visited her grandparents in Ethiopia and seen similar colours on the dresses of villagers dancing the Habesha by the bonfire's light. All that freedom, when happiness and contentment were the knowledge that you had water to drink and sufficient *teff* seed to produce flour and make *injera* over the open fire, its soggy sour presence in your hand wiping and absorbing the last vestige of delicious goat gravy. A different search for happiness had taken over. Tents now gave welcome to Silicone Valley, like the Tika mosquito warping underdeveloped minds.

The cardboard box, now firm between Abrinet's knees, was rekindling Harry's childhood memories. His first tentative sleepover with Gran at the age of six, when there had been ghosts and shadows and unfamiliar sounds. Waking in the night to eerie scratching and ghost-like bleatings coming from the kitchen and hearing the reassurance of Granny getting up and going downstairs to rescue a resuscitated lamb brought frozen and lifeless the night before and placed in a cardboard box next to the warmth of the open Aga door. Revived by warmth, it had scrambled out of the box and was tottering around the kitchen leaving a trail of meconium shit and trying to find succour from a chair leg.

'Good for old Gran, I hope she did have a lover. She deserved one for she understood love. She tried to explain it to me once. I always thought she was holding something back.'

168

'Can you remember her mentioning a Clive?'

'No.'

'Well there's a letter here from his son – it's wonderfully moving, thanking her for giving his father so much joy at the end of his life. I wonder if she confided in anyone. Hang on, there's another note in her hand. It mentions you –shall I read it out?'

Harry stopped what he was doing and stood in the door frame looking down on Abrinet, wanting to hold her and knowing that if he did he would desire something more. She was holding an old Christmas card depicting a wintery scene, trying to decipher the scuffed jottings scribbled over 'Hope to see you in the New Year, love Betty and Fran'. She read: *Shall I tell Harry about Clive – we have always shared our thoughts and he has asked me about love but at fifteen will he understand – could he accept that his Gran in the eyes of the world is having an adulterous affair or will he be disgusted and I would be belittled in his eyes? I feel I must trust him but am uncertain, shall sleep on it.*

Sentayhu was looking up at the unfamiliar faces on the kitchen wall and asking questions, wanting to know their names and what their names meant. Now six years old, he understood that in his mother's culture the names people were given bore significance and he knew that his meant 'What have I been through and what have I seen'.

Abrinet called out to Harry, 'Sen wants to know who all these people are, darling. He says he can remember looking at them once before and holding a very old person's hand when she was in bed. He says it felt bony, like the people in the refugee camps.'

'Be with you in a sec. I'm finding interesting stuff in

Grandfather's study – I think he really loved Gran but was unable to show it. There are little snippets that he has cut out of newspapers and put in an old tin box. He needed the words of others to tell him how he felt about her. Shall I read a couple?'

He started reading before Abrinet answered. 'This must have been in the horoscope section of some newspaper. It says: *Pisces 19 February–19 March*, his birthday was on 15th, curiously enough the Ides of March. It says: *Mercury blowing a kiss to Neptune indicates a lovely moment in a key relationship. This isn't a promise of fireworks, more the recognition that you're with the right person and really wouldn't have it any other way.*'

'How sad. Do you think your grandmother knew? I've just come across a host of notes on the back of old bank statements.' She started reading. '*Poor old Hugh, how he must wish he had married someone else, someone his mother might have approved of. Does he realise his mistake? He has said nothing, he has made his bed and lain on it with me dutifully for sixty-four years, unaware of my unhappiness.*'

Harry leant on the frame of the entrance to his grandfather's study. Still nailed to the door was the rough piece of wood bearing an inscription in Japanese given to him by an Australian POW at the end of the war. He had always told the family that it said Captain's Office but they suspected it said latrine.

Damp and time had taken their toll on the love wall. The cheery, fresh faces from infancy had lost their bloom; their later appearances in university gowns, proud parents in the background, had withered and their faces faded. The dried up Blu-Tack was still trying to hold on but, where it had given up, the corners of those happy memories had curled into shapes which looked like ice-cream cornets and mould had taken over the wall.

The house had been neglected since Julia's death but her presence in it had become stronger. In the preceding years everyone had been too busy and nothing got done. Decisions were pushed to one side, although Matt and Anna kept an eye on the house. But now Harry's uncles, aunts and older cousins were anxious to get on with things, sell the old place because their children and grandchildren were finding it almost impossible to raise a deposit for a bedsit in Clapham. It would make a bomb and probably appear on *Escape to the Country*. But Harry reminded them how Gran had held them all together and none of them wanted to make a move which might make Julia turn in her grave.

It was June when they finally came together again to sort things out. The refugee camps were less demanding as the weather warmed, though this did not lessen Harry and Abrinet's guilt that they were abandoning those in need. Matt and Anna had finished lambing. It would be the first time Matt and Anna had met their daughter-in-law.

'You always said what a strong person your gran was – I'm not so sure. She was pretty vulnerable if these notes are anything to go by.'

'But she always had such a sense of humour, laughing things off. I remember sending her a birthday card when she was eighty-nine and still driving that old car of hers. It said, "My eyesight's gone, my hearing's bad, my joints are stiff and I have trouble staying awake." The punch line over the page said: "Thank God I can still drive!" I can still hear her uncontrolled laughter.'

'There's a long scrawl written on the back of an order form for the Museum Selection Christmas catalogue. I wouldn't have spotted it had I not looked through it. They have some nice things. Shall I read it out?'

'Yep,' Harry replied.

Abrinet half shouted, for Harry had returned to the study. '*Bliss, utter bliss. The sun is shining and my mind is in complete control, happy to drag around the leaden weight of my complaining body. Stood on the backdoor step for hours having a chat with God and watching the clouds changing formation. It's ironic that at this eleventh hour, just as my mind has finally got its act together, my body has capitulated and refuses to cooperate. I fear because of this I shall never meet Abrinet, the love of Harry's life.*' She stopped reading.

Harry poked his head round the door. 'Is that all?'

There were tears rolling down Abrinet's cheeks as she continued reading. '*I hope I was his second love. I wake up early each morning feeling I could move mountains as long as I can get myself safely downstairs. I really must stop buying a newspaper and watching the news, far too depressing. Watched the news last night and am really upset. The French are making heroes out of journalists who denigrate the belief of others. It's a dangerous game to play, to humiliate the sanctity of others for a quick laugh and a quick buck. When someone denigrates Christ I feel pretty sore – I would like to hear what Harry has to say. I am beginning to have a sneaking admiration for Donald Trump and Piers Morgan. Bloody shit, the house is littered with Barclays blue biros and I can't find one. I really must try and drink less.*'

Abrinet wondered what Julia had been doing when she

had felt the need to find a pen and put down her thoughts on paper. The house was still littered with blue biros; they were everywhere like escaping marbles, waiting to be stepped on and send you flying.

She felt a deep sadness that she had never met Julia. Instead of having to try and reassemble Julia's thoughts, they could have discussed things over a cup of coffee and laughed together and remembered when once upon a time there had been an established morality, before laws were made to throw everyone off course and values left unmoored.

Because of its weight, the old leather diary had slipped to the bottom of the box, its scribbled reminders difficult to interpret. 'You told me your grandmother never kept a diary and had confessed to you that she was not sufficiently disciplined. Well, there is one here. There's a thin silk ribbon marking two pages covered in what looks like dried blood.'

Matt and Anna, who had been outside in the barn trying to sort through the mass of vintage farm implements which Hugh had collected, peat spades and horse-driven ploughs, hay turners and milk churns, came into the kitchen hoping for a mug of coffee.

Harry passed the diary to his father. Matt sat on the corner of the table one foot on the floor, like a snooker player obeying rules, and tried to decipher it.

Truly frightening phone call at eight this morning, absolutely vitriolic and malicious. Someone has got it in for Anna.

Matt was quiet for a moment then he said, 'I didn't realised how unhappy my sister was, or what Mum and

173

Gran had to put up with before I was born.'

Abrinet said, 'I didn't know you had a sister, Matt. Harry, you never mention her. Where is she now?'

'She is in a home for alcoholics. Her husband left her, took all the money and is now living on the Costa del Sol. Their son is awaiting trial for fraud. Anna and I tried to help her but we were rejected. We try not to think about it because the memories are too painful, but this incident changed who we all were and shaped our lives. Hate distorts lives.'

Harry returned to the study to go through, yet again, the wartime letters, official documents and photographs of his grandfather, unsure what to keep or if anything had any significance and relevance. Would historians ponder over them or would they not care a fish's tit, an expression he remembered his grandfather using.

Abrinet's said, 'There's one here written on the back of a United Utilities reminder and it mentions you. If I shout can you hear? I'm so warm and cosy here, I don't want to get up.'

'Go ahead.'

'*Am waiting for the recycling team, two cheery young lads with strange hairdos. After much angst and form-filling and a certificate from the doctor to say I have osteoporosis, which I haven't, the council agreed for someone to venture across the cobbles to the back door to collect the mountains of papers which clearing out Hugh's study is producing. Going through his papers makes me realise how fortunate I have been in life and how interesting it has all been, nothing like I imagined it would be. Unplanned, allowing myself to drift along in the bow wave of others – I really have been lucky.* Are you listening, can you hear?' Abrinet who rarely shouted needed to have an answer. She continued reading.

'Harry's mind is a reincarnation of mine so I shall go to my grave contented. Have been meaning to plan my funeral, put my wishes down on paper, show the children I can be organised but haven't yet got down to it – I want it to be joyous, not buried on the high land with Hugh. At the time of his death, the nice young man with the JCB who dug the hole for Hugh kindly asked whether I wanted it double deep so that when the time came I could go on top of him. I never enjoyed being on top. I shall be buried in the small churchyard at the foot of the fells and risk the possibility of landing up next to Mrs. Proudie.

'Why on earth am I feeling so joyous this morning, as though the whole world is on my side? I feel I am about to burst with love for the whole human race but there again it may be that half a bottle of Grouse has disappeared before midday and I shall be left with a headache and guilt. But I would rather have it that way; anyway what is guilt? Most of it is imposed upon you by others.

'Was that the moment when I was first made to encounter guilt. Caught by my grandmother at six years old, squatting on my haunches, having a desperate pee, letting go with relief onto that small patch of hidden soil under the wooden steps which joined the nursery on the second floor to the conservatory, where nothing grew other than groundsel and nettles. Was that where the seed corn of my guilt was sown, in that secret hiding place of childhood?'

Sen joined his father in his great-grandfather Hugh's study. Together they looked at the rows of medals. Harry wished he had listened more closely to what they all were. He said to Sen, 'We can look them up on the internet.'

They both felt so close to Hugh, as though he were still there. His war would soon be forgotten in order to make way for new wars. Sen asked, 'Why do men go to war?'

But nobody could tell him; he was asking the same question his father, grandfather and great-grandfather had asked – and Julia was still asking.

Abrinet picked up another card with a painting of honeysuckle on the front under which was written a familiar quote, a cliché much loved of the card-producing industry. Julia's strong hand covered the back; it was undated.

Harry is with me today, what joy. Unlike his cousins, he never needs to be entertained so I never mind looking after him. As it was fine and I feel spring is finally here, have given him the job pulling out the sycamore seedlings before the soil gives them that iron grip which makes removing them without a spade impossible. He's counting each one and has got to 287. The sun has brought the dandelions out in their thousands. Why is it that we persecute them but welcome primroses and daffodils? It's like ethnic cleansing.

Harry heard Abrinet laughing and came through. Unable to resist touching her, he bent down and kissed her head and they read the message together.

The card felt thick as though it contained something else; the back and front were held together by something sticky that looked like congealed fat. Abrinet pulled it apart. A photo of a small boy fell out, striding purposely, clutching a fistful of sycamore seedlings. Written on the back: *My all-time favourite photo of Harry – so conscientious, confident but so, so vulnerable.*

Harry said, 'I remember that day well – it was the first time I had stayed for a sleepover on my own.'

He sat down beside her on the floor. The box looked empty, but he saw wedged beneath the flaps of cardboard at the bottom what looked like an income tax demand. Julia's familiar hand covered the questionnaire on the reply side.

Today I did something reprehensible and I don't really know why. A wasp came into the kitchen. It was doing me no harm but fear of what it might do made me look for a newspaper with which to swat it, I couldn't find one, they had all been recycled but found instead the remains of a fly killer spray and instead of swatting it and giving it a quick decisive death I sprayed it. Initially I thought it had escaped the chemical but within a minute it began to behave like an aeroplane out of control, twisting and turning until finally it lay on the table in front of me, arching its back like a contortionist, flipping, spinning like a gyroscope acting out its macabre death dance. I should have squashed it, put it out of its misery, but to my shame I watched it for thirty minutes, hypnotised by its death throes until its movements finally stopped and it put out its sting in a final act of defiance.

There was silence then Abrinet said, 'I have watched children die in a similar way.'

Harry took her hand and pulled her to her feet. He said, 'Let's get finished here. We need to get back.'

Lightning Source UK Ltd.
Milton Keynes UK
UKOW05f0019291016
286428UK00007B/44/P